Flora's Wreath

Jane Dill

Flora's Wreath

ILDOLYN
PRESS

Friday Harbor, WA

Second Printing

Ildolyn Press
Friday Harbor, WA 98250

Cover design by Alice Shull
Interior layout and publishing services by W. Bruce Conway

Printed in the U.S.A. on recycled paper

Soft cover   ISBN: 978-0-9830605-0-5
Hard cover ISBN: 978-0-9830605-1-2
eBook   ISBN: 978-0-9830605-2-9

Library of Congress Control Number: 2010917411

To Charlie

In the United States, terminally ill residents of three states have access to legal means of ending their lives.

Oregon was the first to establish, by means of voter approval in a 1994 general election, their Death With Dignity Act.

Washington State voters approved a Death With Dignity law in 2008 – Initiative 1000.

Montana established legality through its Montana State Supreme Court ruling, on December 31, 2009, in favor of Baxter v. Montana. Ironically, Mr. Baxter died on the same day as the initial lower court ruling in his favor, December 5, 2008, without realizing the outcome of his action.

The Gift

The Gift

Medicared, socially secured, and bureaucratically crammed into a pigeonhole labeled senior citizen – my sixty-fifth birthday was a bit of a bust. Pleasant enough, with customary congratulations and luncheon with friends, it was still a day that left me longing for the hoopla of my childhood. In my earlier days, birthday parties were not the organized events held at bowling alleys and pizza parlors for today's youngsters. No, our mothers staged our home-place extravaganzas, God help them, and invariably our crepe paper festooned parties turned into raucous affairs despite their strident efforts to contain us. We raced with potatoes carried in spoons, cheated at blind man's bluff and pinned donkey tails on anything that got in our way, to excited shrieks of delight and warning. Eventually the downtown movie man would come with his silvered screen, and we settled down to enter Darla and Spanky's world while our mothers retreated to the dining room, and drank martinis out of tea-cups.

I wanted it back again, all of it - birthday cake with that extra candle to 'grow on', Neapolitan ice cream with its lusted-for strawberry stripe, being the birthday-girl and not 'having to share' for one glorious day. I longed to feel again the delicious experience of misbehaving with abandon and without consequence. I wanted to step through the dubious comfort of my present day cocoon and frolic unrestrained by the barnacles of my years. Having miraculously moved beyond thirty years of an implosive marriage to a very different life, I was now retired, sixty-five, and found myself longing to be six.

I was knee-deep in a bona fide funk, and I don't do funks gracefully.

This persistent state of unrest lasted throughout the day no matter how I tried to jolly myself out of it. A disturbing sensation, like a flickering eyelash 'butterfly kiss', appeared from time to time next to my left earlobe, and it ruffled an interred memory. What was it that was attempting to surface? I tried to reason with myself. Nothing extraordinary aside from my having lived to this age was going to happen this day, I insisted, and actually, nothing did. But, as my 65th birthday dipped toward twilight, the restlessness I had experienced since waking that morning began to take hold. I found myself becoming entangled in the web of premonition, incapable of detachment. The sensation at my earlobe became more and more pronounced.

So, I did what I had long ago found essential when my inner cosmos becomes aroused. I centered myself, and waited for whatever it was that had already begun.

———

The bong-bong-bong of my chimes, when they sounded early that evening, prompted me to drop the dishtowel from the wineglass I was mechanically polishing. It was too late for deliveries. I certainly wasn't expecting anyone else to drop by. Carefully, while listening for another sounding of the chimes, I set the glass on the counter and bent to retrieve the towel from my kitchen floor. The second set of bongs followed fast on the first, and I turned with heightened senses toward their old N-B-C tune.

Stepping without feeling in my feet through the hallway, sucking in my stomach while taking a deep breath, I grasped the glass knob of my front door and abruptly opened it - to find a purple suited stranger standing on my front porch. The short, round woman who smiled up at me through a slightly protruding overbite looked, for all the world, like a character out of a storybook. Even in her heeled pumps she barely reached my shoulder. High cheekbones rose roundly beneath crinkly eyes of a color I couldn't properly see. A professional's touch had given her graying curls a blended soft coppery shade that most likely had been hers in youth; also her eyebrows, full and un-plucked, displayed the same rusty tone. Manicured nails were painted to complement her hair and, tucked in next to her waist and held close by her elbow, she carried a brown-papered parcel about the size of a telephone book.

And, dear God, she was haloed. By some penumbral trick of evening fog and streetlight a misty, golden glow surrounded her entire head, which made her unexpected appearance at my doorway even more dramatic. I stood there, literally awestruck. For a moment I was dumbstruck as well, before I rather bluntly asked who she was, and whether there was something special that brought her to my door.

Her voice, when she spoke, carried a slight sibilance.

"I have come," she announced in what sounded to me a practiced tone, "to deliver your final gift of the day. It has been waiting a rather long time for this occasion, and I have trav-eled here from Philadelphia that I might present it to you in person."

With that introduction of sorts, she proffered her business card from which I learned her name, Lydia Wharen, and that she was affiliated, as partner, with a Philadelphia law firm. I looked down at her with even more curiosity. We were a long way from Pennsylvania. At this juncture, I glanced beyond her haloed head and observed a dark limousine parked at my curb, lights extinguished, silently waiting to retrieve this woman once her task had been performed. Chauffeured, manicured, lettered in law – not quite commonplace, I mused, for a cou-rier. But in some odd way, I realized, this was a perfectly appro-priate ending to my sixty fifth year.

"Surprising as my appearance must be to you," my caller said as she looked up into my face, "I confess to a puzzlement of my own. I know who you are, and a bit about your maternal family background, but, of course, I am totally unknown to you. If you will allow us a time to visit, I will explain, as best I can, how I came to be involved in this odd presentation. I could do with a sit down and a strong drink, as a matter of fact," she offered with a little laugh.

As could I.

Even though I had been definitely taken aback by the appearance of this woman at my door, standing aside for her to enter my home instinctively seemed the most natural thing to do. I was greatly relieved to find that as Lydia Wharen, Esq. walked through my foyer, her halo had been left behind. I casually noticed a dip to Lydia's left shoulder as she passed, accompanied by a slight limp on that same side, and briefly wondered as to the cause. When we entered my living room, I also detected a well-worn kind of weariness, and surmised that my guest's affliction, whatever it was, had been incorporated into her life a long time ago.

Prepared to suggest that she rest a bit, I was offset by Lydia's keen interest in a tour of what I lovingly term my funky house. Now, normally I would not dream of taking a perfect stranger into my home, let alone conduct one through it, but tonight was already way beyond normal; consequently, I found myself leading Lydia across my alder floors with their rosewood butterfly-joins to show her the trompe l'oiel paintings on my doors. She clapped her hands in delight when she saw the buckshot that years ago had struck the barn whose sides now panel my kitchen. As we returned to the living room, where I passed to the wet-bar for glasses, Glenlivet, and ice, Lydia Wharen, Esq. began to lose her status as stranger.

A questioning look as I raised the bottle brought a decisive nod of approval from my guest. She had perched herself atop two cushions on my large leather sofa, and was now observing me studiously. In turn I gazed straight back at her as I poured a good measure of scotch over ice cubes, and passed her glass across the old trunk that serves as my coffee table. Finally, I noticed, Lydia had released the package to which she had been attached since her arrival. It now sat beside her, a mystery within its wrappings, as this new acquaintance of mine casually removed her plum colored pumps and proceeded to further surprise me. Seated as she was, Lydia looked remarkably like the hookah-smoking caterpillar atop his mushroom in Alice's underworld, and she dangled toes whose pedicured tips had been stroked by a brush dipped in brilliant royal blue polish.

"A secret amusement of mine," she claimed as she noticed me staring, "rather like wearing racy underwear. I sometimes think, when appearing in my professional capacity, 'If only my clients and adversaries could see my little painted piggies!' They have silently amused me through many a sober conference," she laughed.

Through no willing act of my own I found myself beginning to like this woman. A bonding that we each realized and acknowledged at the same moment by an involuntary intake of breath had imperceptibly begun. From her cushioned position, and my seated one, we savored a few moments of reflection along with our scotch. While I swirled ice through amber liquid, Lydia fingered the twine that protected the final gift of my sixty-fifth year, toying with the bindings of my years to come.

Time took a seat and waited while, for those few moments, we simply regarded each other without speaking.

Then Lydia stretched, repositioned those blue tipped toes beneath her and drank to our futures, wondering whether they might in some ways be intertwined. We could not have begun to imagine, from our odd beginning, what our lives still held in store. She began to explain the reason for her unexpected arrival. I found her voice pleasantly intriguing, and listened without interruption as she unwound the tale of her connection to the parcel at her side.

"When I was eight years old," Lydia began her story, "I was stricken with infantile paralysis. My personal sunlight was extinguished while I lived in a shaded room. Faces around me were forcedly optimistic, waiting for whatever was to happen as we traveled through my illness. Apart from all the care I was given at that time, both medical and familial, what mattered most to me in my shrunken world was being left behind in school. Staying back, while my classmates went on without me was, to me, at least as catastrophic as infantile paralysis itself. During those days, no tutor would come to the house of someone with Sister Kenny's disease, and my mother was not especially well herself. Even as I speak to you now, I feel a throwback to that time," she said with a slight shake of her head.

Lydia paused a moment or two before continuing, while she collected thoughts from among her memories.

"But the gods were tuned in to my fears," she went on, "for unbeknownst to me there was someone who would become my lifetime ally. I had always distantly known my grandfather as a kind man who read books, drank old-fashioneds with cherries in them, and smoked cigars. He was a man too wrapped up in his work, I was told, to take time for anyone outside his courtroom, excepting, of course, my grandmother Bridey. Well, Grandfather made time for me. He had always fondly called me 'Princess', and he now became my personal Knight-in-Shining-Armor. We covered my assigned schoolwork as quickly as we could, when he arrived at the end of his day; then he would whisk me away, taking me on amazing journeys with Jules Vern or Lucius Beebe, or through the looking glass with Alice. During the long months of my recovery I became familiar with Shakespeare's works, thanks to Grandfather's introduction of Charles and Mary Lamb, and I loved imagining myself as Portia. My grandfather's companionship, and his determination to have me move beyond the boundaries of my room, opened doors to limitless landscapes of imagination. The misfortune of my illness led to a lifetime bond with this incredibly gifted man," she said in a voice laden with love.

Lydia paused, looked into the bottom of her glass, and extended it in request for a refill. This I gladly gave, along with more ice and a splash of soda, but I did not join her this time.

I had had enough for the day, and did not want to miss a word of what was yet to be said. Also, I noticed for the first time as she turned the parcel over, daubs of deep green sealing wax on the package still at her side, and they precipitated a memory shift within me. My attention wavered as Lydia again took up her tale.

"As my strength returned, "she went on, "I began questioning Grandfather about the work he did. Delighted with my interest, he began to explain his profession in ways that an eight-year-old child could grasp. He created courtrooms in which we both assumed parts; we were witnesses, jurors, bailiffs, accused and accuser, and finally I was permitted to play Portia. But only Grandfather was allowed to be the judge. Within and without our fabricated environs, this position was his alone.

By the time I was healthy enough to leave that imaginary world behind, I had decided that law was the real world I wanted to enter when I grew up. My personal alliance with my grandfather ultimately became a professional one, as well. Much of my work today is done on behalf of injured or disabled people, for my own limitations connect them to me, and seem to sway juries in their behalf. It still humbles me to realize the unforseen outcomes of my dark times."

Lydia slid from her cushioned position on the sofa to its seat, then stood on the carpet in her stocking feet. I briefly thought how I must run down to the drug store for some glitzy polish of my own - maybe orange, with sparkles! She walked the length of the room, stretched both arms and body by bending and touching her own fancy toes, then straightened and walked slowly back, speaking as she returned. I contemplated snatching up the abandoned package while she was away from it, but harnessed my thoughts and let my gift remain on the sofa. I imagined her in a courtroom as she came toward me, glad that I wasn't facing her in one.

⸺

"All of what I have told you is background for the reason I am here with you tonight," Lydia said, somehow reading my wish for her to get on with it. "I know, I know," she resumed as she patted my gift. "It is already yours, but please, bear with me just a bit longer, as I really need to tell you about my involvement in all of this. In some strange way, it is hard for me to give up this bundle, a last tangible link to my grandfather, I suspect," Lydia sighed, as she resettled herself on the sofa.

"On the day that I became a partner in my grandfather's law firm," Lydia's ending began, "the Judge summoned me into his office and exacted a promise from me. Given that you and I were both alive, this package would be delivered, by me, to you, on your sixty-fifth birthday. If you had not achieved this day, it was to be incinerated without its contents being revealed. Had I died before today, my son would be here with you now. All I know of your gift," as she stroked its wrappings, "is that it was entrusted to my grandfather, shortly before her death, by a friend he admired beyond words. At the time it was given into his hands, he and my grandmother lived in a little town near the Poconos, where he had first practiced law, and he cared deeply enough for this friend to honor her request without question. This mystery," she looked down briefly to her side, " has rested in his personal safe for nearly fifty years. When I unlocked that safe this morning, it sat in lone splendor, knowing its time had arrived."

As she handed her charge to me, Lydia studied my reaction while I turned my gift from back to front. I know not what my face revealed, but was again thankful that I wasn't on a witness stand before her. Recognition and impossibility held sway, as I felt my birthday present warm and pulse in my hands.

An exquisitely drawn wreath adorned with four perfectly detailed flowers and several little blue ones; the hand that had penned 'Janeylib' in her calligraphic style; the seals of wax that bore her monogram: Flora, my Great Aunt Flora, dead since I

was twenty, began her return to my world. I can claim aston-
ishment, but not total disbelief as to what was happening, for
Flora's magic began intertwining with my own long before I
can remember.

———

Lydia Wharen was innately aware of the shift of ener-
gies in the room. She knew that her mission had been accomplished. Her promise, made so long ago, had been kept.

"Lydia," I questioned as she rose to leave, "the Pennsylvania town in which your grandparents lived - was it, by any
chance, the town of White Laurel?"

"It was, and is," she replied as she slipped into her shoes.
"My interest in your final gift of the day does not match your
own, but it has been a fascination to me for thirty seven years.
Philadelphia is simply a phone call and a few hours' flight time
away," she assured me. "I suspect that this visit has, for us, been
more than just an introduction. For my own part, Janeylib, I
sincerely hope so."

With that short leave-taking, Lydia, the lady of the night,
was gone. Her small, round silhouette slipped into the dark
interior of her waiting limousine, off to the night sky for her
journey home.

———

Except for my Great Aunt Flora, no one until now had
called me Janeylib. Flora's voice swirled silently, drifting against
my ear, while her gift lay warm in my lap.

Seeing her pet name for me now, penned by her hand,
and holding that hand in my own after so many years of longing to do so, brought all of my present senses plunging toward
a deep, central core.

Huge, invisible doors were sequentially closed around me.
Sounds were not muffled or far away – no, nothing such as that;
sound simply ceased to exist. The world, my world, was still out
there, while I became part of an entirely separate one. Physically rooted, I was nonetheless transported, emptied, rendered

mute, and motionless. I became heavier, more dense, shorter in stature. Time, in its wisdom, watched from the sidelines, while gentle waves of energy worked their way through my body. For some time I simply sat, knowing I could move, but not moving.

Then, little by little, awareness of my place in this world resumed. Normal height and weight gradually returned. Fingers pulsed, flexed, and relaxed their grip on Flora's gift. I heard a dog in mid bark, and the tire sounds of a passing car indicated that it had been raining.

Nothing was different. Everything had changed.

Like a pearl inside its oyster, shelled with brown paper and tied by forty-nine-year-old jute, this gift from beyond the edges of the unknown rested in my lap. An exquisitely drawn wreath holding four blossoms and a scattering of small blue flowers absorbed my gaze. I held it reverently, sniffing it to try to catch a bit of her fragrance. Finally, in awe and with unhurried care, I loosened each of the two grateful knots, tied more than half my lifetime ago. The pair of wax seals then yielded, one by one, to the heated knife slipped beneath them, sighing with gratitude as their task of containment ended. As I folded back the outer wrappings, then did the same with two layers of white tissue, I saw for the first time my great aunt Flora's legacy.

Soft leather tenderly bound pristine pages of white, each of them bearing the unmistakable calligraphy of Flora's hand. As her words exposed themselves to my eyes, my great aunt invisibly billowed into the room, suffusing the space around me with traces of her presence. My teacher, my friend, my guide to the unknowable, dead these past forty-five years, had begun her journey back into life.

My decision to present Flora's tale to others' eyes has not

been made in haste, for it is fraught with secrets perhaps best left untold. It was Flora's wreath itself, that nesting of green that forever holds Camas, Iris, Daphne, and Lily in its protective embrace, that begged me to do so. It is coiled of rosemary, the herb of remembrance.

———

Be with me now, as I tell of my great aunt, and read what Flora has to say.

Flora

Flora was a person who lived reluctantly in this world, having never quite left the one from which she had come. She learned to manage both realms quite well, but balancing them, especially when she was a young girl, she told me, was often difficult. It gives me pause to imagine how her personality might be judged by today's criteria. In her time – she was born in the mid-1870s – she was appropriately considered to have an artist's temperament, and wisely was left to establish her own patterns.

Her love affair with the outdoors became both anchor and sail to Flora. As a girl, she often walked the Pennsylvania woods near her home, always with notebooks ready to receive her drawings of mushrooms, plants, and the furry or feathered creatures she encountered. As Flora matured, so did the quality of the work accomplished on her now daily hikes. Her drawings were not only anatomically accurate, they also coaxed the viewer's eye into the inner life of the subjects she portrayed. Flora saw soul in everything, especially in rocks.

Gradually, Flora grew more comfortable and trusting of the world around her, and by the time she reached young womanhood, the works done during her forays into the forest had become a considerable portfolio. Her impressive illustrations, plus the fact that I am sure she charmed her interviewers, led to Flora's acceptance into the Pennsylvania Academy of the Fine Arts in Philadelphia, when she was just seventeen years old. This institution, she was forever happy to include in conversation, was the very first of its kind in our country. Rightfully delighted by her admission into their programs of study,

Flora entered the academy and flourished within the demanding discipline of applying learned techniques to her own work. One of three women admitted, she became unique among them by securing future employment prior to her graduation. Her portrayals of wildflowers, beautifully colored and exquisitely detailed, captured the interest of her professor of botany. His desire to enlist Flora as illustrator of his forthcoming book, *Wildflowers of the Poconos,* led to the first of her employments as a botanical illustrator. No longer in print, this book is nonetheless highly valued today as a source of reference. My own signed copy is a personal treasure.

By the time my great aunt was twenty-two years old, her reputation as a botanical illustrator was becoming well regarded. With mixed feelings of longing and relief, Flora told me she had begun planning her future around being a self-sufficient maiden lady for the rest of her days. This was a state that she willingly embraced. Such, however, was not to be her destiny.

Harry Norris, the young doctor who had attended Flora's coming into the world, had waited those twenty-two years for Flora to become the woman he had oddly foreseen at her birth. It was her eyes, he later told his bride, that had captured him. Just born, Flora had the knowledge of the spheres in her eyes; they had plunged into his soul, captured it, and never left. Twenty-six years her senior, and a dear friend to Flora's father, Dr. Norris somehow gained consent to court his friend's daughter. How, Flora had mused, she would never know.

My great aunt had never thought fondly of marriage. The bonds of matrimony were to her just that – bonds, and ties that bind were frightening things. As far as marriage being an institution, so were prisons and asylums, and she had no wish to commit herself. If one desired children, she conceded, marriage had its merits. Flora did not want to bear children, and she had considered a single life the one way to assure that she was safe from doing so. She thoroughly enjoyed her friendships with men, but refused their proposals of marriage.

But, here was Dr. Norris, whom she had known and admired forever. In turn, Harry Norris had long appreciated the gifts of the woman he loved, and valued the work she was inspired to do. There was no question, on his part, of Flora's continuing her projects after their marriage. He simply expected that she would do so. He further defied the convention of his day by traveling to Philadelphia, and staying overnight, in order to be with her. They spent long hours walking the pathways of Fairmount Park, listening to and learning from each other and, for Flora, falling in love. When she, as she knew she must, expressed her determination on the subject of bearing children, Harry had audibly let forth a sigh of relief. She had echoed his personal views on procreation, he told her, to the immense joy and relief of them both. As a doctor, he assured her, he could promise a stellar conjugal life without fear of consequence. When he opened his arms and heart to her, Flora entered his embrace and lived for years within its warmth. The man who attended her first birth, she told me, was responsible for the second, as well.

—— ~—

Harry Norris, M.D. took down his shingle on the day that Flora agreed to combine her life with his, thus ending his years of medical practice and beginning his long awaited life with Flora. Twelve years was the span of time allotted them; a lifetime, during which they traveled both in this country and abroad, and built the wonderful Norris Gardens that survives them both today.

On one of their several trips to Yellowstone National Park, she actually met President Theodore Roosevelt when he and Harry sat in rockers together at Old Faithful Inn, smoked cigars, and talked of big game hunting. Harry's own foray into hunting, much to her relief, was confined to the search and collection of new specimens for Norris Gardens. Harry's personal interest leaned toward plants which held medicinal value, and wandered further to those that were, as he termed it, suspicious. Always taken with them on their journeys was a large steamer trunk, fitted especially to house and coddle transplants going to their new homes in White Laurel. Holes were drilled into the trunk's sides and lid, while its face displayed a series of specifically fitted drawers that could be unlocked and withdrawn, allowing individual care for plants in transit. Today, those drawers house old Parcheesi parts and Dominos in my living room.

Collected, catalogued and transferred to paper by Flora's drawings, plants hitherto unknown to Pennsylvania were meticulously recorded. Tended on arrival in the hothouse nursery that still occupies a corner of the Doctor's separate garden, survival rate of the newcomers was extraordinary. Several descendants live today within the confines of that fenced and gated garden, where all but he and Flora were denied entry. In the months before Flora's death, I was invited into that space, and accompanied my great aunt in the destruction of much that grew there.

———

I need to speak a bit here of the gardens built by Harry, Flora, and members of the Floraphile Horticultural Society. It contains nine-foot hexagonal beds stitched together by bands of wooly and elfin thymes, and it spreads a floral quilt patterned after Grandmother's Flower Garden atop five acres of land. Perennials have their places in each of these hexagons, but it is the annuals diligently planted and dug by Floraphile volunteers that supply an ever-changing panoply of color. During each season, a new quilt appears. In the central hexagon, at the heart of the garden, a dwarf Japanese maple tree is nourished with the ashes of the two who planted it there. Someday the red lacey-leafed tree will know my ashes as well.

———

The lucky land that supports this horticultural counterpane is also home to the mansard-roofed Victorian house that once held Harry's medical offices, and was home for him and his bride. A tour of Norris Gardens includes an optional climb to the once-forbidden sunroom on the third floor. It is well worth making the effort, for it is from this heightened vantage point that the quilted pattern of the gardens truly emerges.

———

And I will disclose a secret once shared by Flora and me. There are fairies that visit the heart of this garden. It was one of them at my ear on my birthday, an almost forgotten messenger from my past.

———

Describing Flora is a challenge, but I will try. Words can paint a picture, I know, so I shall use my writer's brush to bring her to the printed page.

My great aunt had the appearance of being a dainty woman, which she was not. Strands of soft, white hair escaped the confines of a bun shaped on top of her head, crossed her high forehead, and caressed the lines of her face. Her feet always seemed to be elevated from the ground by an imperceptible layer of air, for she moved the way that sea foam does across the sands, skimming the surface as it darts about seeking purchase. Her complexion was similar in color to a rosy cambric tea, a shade I attributed at the time to her hours spent in the great outdoors. I have since done research on our family's lineage, and have discovered a delicious mix of bloodlines.

One would have termed Flora's eyes a light, sparkling blue, and so they were. But, their color was deepened by unbidden shifts of mood; opalescent flecks of gold and green flashed and faded according to her inner tides. Most memorable of all is that, like the sea, Flora's eyes could be entered. Not without invitation, of course, and not without reciprocity.

During my eighth summer, while seated with my great

aunt beside the young Japanese maple, I felt the encompassing gaze of Flora's eyes surrounding, beckoning me, and I tumbled freely into them. I found myself engulfed, suspended inside my great aunt, slowly rising and sinking within the essence of her being. No sense of Time was with me, as I drifted lazily through softened colors and subdued sound, ever so slowly propelled past places where secrets were held. I was suffused with warmth and a profound sense of total comfort, as she flowed in and I flowed out. Finally, with unhurried levitation, I rose from within that unfamiliar world, and found myself once again looking into her remarkable eyes. They were shining from a face alive with love. She too, had had a journey.

———

Teacher and friend, my great aunt Flora was my guide to finding the stepping-stones along life's rocky roadway.

Flora

Flora's Legacy

❧

Welcome to your sixty sixth year of life, Janeylib. You, my solemn child, did not think that you would live long enough to reach this birthday. Have you yet come to appreciate that you still have a future; that life continues to open until it closes? Feel the fear of your own unknown, my love, and walk through the opened doorways anyway. We did, and our worlds were forever expanded.

Both legacy and gift, these pages that you now hold are one of my major efforts, and also one of my last, as I am approaching my own journey on the train to Glory. The pages hold many stories, but only one central core, and they will introduce you to three ordinary, remarkable women. Peopled also in the pages are those with, and for whom, we worked. They are the forget-me-nots in your little wreath, tucked in near the blossoms you see. The four of us, Lily, Iris, Daphne, and myself, are the blossoms, mine being the Camas flower. We agreed, shortly after we began our mission, that someday our tale should be told, and the task has fallen to me, as I had hoped it would. You will be the first, again by group agreement, to see into our lives and determine our futures.

Soon, you will begin to understand why this package has slumbered so long in solitude, safely tucked away from view. Now, like the Beauty you loved hearing about, it is time that these pages receive the kiss of your true love. All of the people who are about to become known to you will have joined me in death, as will have their partners. Even the children with whom some of us have gifted the world will, most likely, have died. No one will be left to suffer the repercussions that surely would have befallen us all, had our activities become exposed. Hopefully, by the time you are reading this, the world will have changed in its attitudes toward ministrations such as ours.

———

And so I begin, with introductions.

Flora's Legacy

Camas

Camas

We found it rather fun, the four of us, to assume floral names when we began the Floraphile Horticultural Society. I chose 'Camas', as Harry had likened me to his favorite northwestern wildflower. I was his wild flower, he told me, and he also said that the blue of my eyes matched the color of the camas flower. When picked, this little flower quickly loses its petals. 'Rather like you, my dear one; best to leave it undisturbed, and let it grow,' was my husband's observation. He knew me so well.

We encountered vast fields of these little blue blossoms during our first trip to Yellowstone Park, and learned that Indians had cultivated many acres of *camassia quamash*, as they harvested their bulbs for food. Even more interesting to both Harry and me is the white plumed cousin of the blue camas flower – not recommended as an edible vegetable, for your first bite of the 'death camas' will be your last. We returned with a quantity of bulbs from both varieties for Harry's personal garden. They were among our most successful transplants.

———

My friends have asked to be known only through the horticultural identities chosen by each of them. However, I have neither need nor desire for anonymity, so to avoid confusion will, from now on, refer to myself as Flora throughout these pages. Now, daughter of my heart, I shall introduce you to the three women who are represented in your little wreath. Together, we welcome you into our circle.

Daphne

Daphne

Lily and Iris I have known since childhood, while Daphne, with her sunset curls, came to town when she was fifteen. I was by then in my early twenties, home for a visit with my parents when this wisp of a girl arrived at our house one morning, her arms laden with dahlias and roses. Her mother and father, so I thought then, had been recent dinner guests of my parents, and Daphne had been sent to deliver the flowers as a lovely token of thanks for the evening they had spent. She passed me as I sat on the lawn sketching the ethereal blossoms of Queen Anne's lace. I remember thinking that Daphne's own coloring, the soft blush of her cheeks and sprinkle of freckles across them, along with her wonderful red hair, eclipsed the palette of the bouquet she carried. She really is remarkably pretty.

After leaving the flowers with our maid, she stopped awhile to watch as I worked, and inquired as to the wee deep purple one at the center of Queen Anne's group of flowers. I related the story that this is the spot most attractant to bees, and that after their visit and subsequent pollination, the surrounding flowers curl inward to protect their fertilized blossom. Intrigued, Daphne lingered with more questions, and answers to some of mine. Our friendship began that August day, and like the pollinated blossom of Queen Anne's lace, it has enclosed and protected its precious center ever since.

I did ask Daphne to write her own story, but she declined. 'You can tell it so much better, Flora,' she laughed. But, I cannot. So here, as best I can recall them, are her words as she spoke them to me.

"We left the land where I was born," Daphne began, "my Mam, Gran, and I, when I was a young child, but there are things I still remember about my birthplace. Ireland is thought by people in this country to be all green and shining, and they call it the Emerald Isle. Well, it was not that way to me. What I remember most, color-wise, is gray - in all its many shades. Although we were certainly very poor, I don't recall feeling less fortunate than anyone else, nor was I generally unhappy. We were not as hungry as many, for we had a small garden, and my mother could make soup out of air, it seemed. However, times were hard and getting harder. My father had died, or left. I have never really been told which. It was a subject that neither my mother nor grandmother cared to talk about. Gran was actually my paternal grandmother, had lived with us since before I was born, and she adored me. One morning I woke up to find suitcases by the door. Seanene, my doll that Gran had made for me, with hair redder than mine, was lying on top of the satchel meant for me.

We were sailing to America! I remember being frightened of leaving all that I had ever known, as I was carried along, but I had no time to think about it. 'It will be fine. It will be an adventure. It will be a better life for us all.' These assurances were made to me again and again by my mam. There were other people on the ship traveling with children, sailing for this foreign land, and it began to be fun. For the greater part, it was an adventure! I had a grand time on the voyage and I never once got sick at my stomach, which made me feel very much the sailor," Daphne laughed. " Later, I could only wonder how my mother and grandmother were able to assure themselves during this journey of theirs. Strong women, each of them, it still took some amazing quality to step from the edge of the world they knew and sail off into the unknown, especially with a child in tow. How truly brave they were."

Daphne rested at this point in her telling, lost within the wash of her own recollections. She sat quietly, hands cupped one within the other on her lap. We waited for stirred memories to once again find a comfortable resting spot, while she gazed beyond, to a place far from where we were sitting. Time waited. Then, looking directly at me, Daphne softly said, "Thank you, Flora. I don't believe that I have ever spoken this way before. It is good having them with me again."

———

After another few minutes, Daphne went on, her voice less subdued. "Without my knowing, when we were still in Ireland, my mother had signed papers in order to become an indentured servant to a family in Massachusetts. This is how we were admitted to America. My grandmother had insisted on coming to our new country with us, and had also agreed to serve for a seven-year period. It was a position that she did not live long enough to fill. The Boston household that hired them had agreed to employ both women, and to accept me, as well. I realize today that this was most unusual, but so was the entire household we had blindly joined.

"We were what was called 'common Irish'," Daphne went on, "a group looked down upon at that time by many people in America, and especially so by 'lace curtain Irish'. We were servants, all of us, as I was expected to perform tasks suitable to my age, and we were obviously poor, practically penniless, bound no matter what to this household, these people, for seven years. Legally, I was not bound, but to all intents and purposes, I was. We were literally at the mercy of our employers.

They were of German and English descent. Her family had arrived in this country from England in the time of Cromwell, while his parents had left Germany the year before he was born. He owned and ran a factory begun by his father that manufactured leather shoes and boots. She ran the household, supervised their five children, did charity work, and dyed her hair."

Daphne paused, poured herself some tea, repositioned herself in the Morris chair, and resumed her story.

"Mam had been hired as cook, and Gran as kitchen help. They were both agog at the size of 'their' kitchen and its equip- ment, to say nothing of the variety and supply of foods avail- able to them. My mother, already a good cook, soon proved herself a superb one. Together, she and Gran became respon- sible for the most eagerly attended dinner parties in Boston. I could fill several books with stories of those years, but needn't fill yours with them. What I do need to say is that I had no way of knowing then how the luck of the Irish had befallen us. Within two years, indentures were rescinded for both Mam and Gran. They were, we were, free, to go wherever we chose to go. We chose to stay. Actually, in a way, I am still there."

"Now, Flora," Daphne said as she sat straighter in her chair, "I come to one of the most important parts in what I am telling you this afternoon, and you must forgive my probable tears."

Daphne got up, and strolled away from her chair before turning and speaking from where she stood, while I sat with notebook in lap, waiting to record what she had to tell.

——

"Among the ages of our employers' five children," she said before returning to her seat, "my own registered somewhere in the middle. The two older boys and their sister, who was about my age, went daily to Llewellyn Academy, while the two young- er children received lessons from their governess. One morning - I shall never forget that day - as I was carrying linens to the laundry, I stopped to listen at the door of the nursery, where the little ones were hearing stories and being coaxed to read. And I was caught. Scared to death that I would be punished, or banished, or both, I ran to the laundry in tears, dropped the linens, and turned to run toward the comfort of the kitchen. Again, I was caught. The Mistress had followed, and stood in the doorway, fully occupying the space between me and any chance of escape. I was terrified. Then, Flora," Daphne said as if still in awe, "she stooped before me, took my frightened face in her cool hands, looked at me with unexpected kindness, and asked words which changed my life. 'Would you like to learn, child?'

I simply gulped through my tears as I nodded, and that was enough. I started lessons the very next day, with permission and gratitude from my astonished mother. Within the year I was placed in the same school as the older children. On my first day there, accompanied by Mam and the Mistress, I could not understand my mother's beaming face and streaming eyes."

Daphne paused a bit here, and her next words came from an even deeper place within her.

"That singular windfall has determined my entire life, Flora," Daphne said. "I had no idea then how utterly unheard of it is to educate the child of one's servants. My benefactors, for that is what they truly were, regarded their act as if it were entirely commonplace. I used to imagine who or where I would be today without benefit of my education. I don't do that anymore. It is unthinkable."

"Over the years, Mam had many offered opportunities to work for more money than she was currently earning. Never once did she even consider accepting one of them. Of all the acts of equalization done by our employers (they eventually refused to be termed 'employers' and insisted on being addressed by their names), their educating me glued Mam to them forever. When fire destroyed the shoe factory, the family's fortune was drastically reduced, and resulted in the sale of the Boston mansion and our move to White Laurel. As I mentioned earlier," Daphne said with a sly smile, " in a way, I am still with the family I knew then. My James is the second of their two older boys, and the house in which we now live is the one we first came to from Boston."

Iris

Iris

We were babies together, Iris and I. She preceded me into this world by seven months and four days, and never let me forget that she was 'my elder', but later in our lives I turned the tables on that one! Our families lived on the same street and the two of us shared absolutely everything, including the measles and chicken pox. Pennsylvania porches practically perch on the sidewalks, and we used to climb out our bedroom windows onto porch-roofs to haughtily look down on the people passing below, convinced that they could not see us. We were sure that we could stick out our tongues and make ugly faces in safety! On summer evenings we sat and watched the stars come out, if we could coax a mother to come out onto the roof with us. That was almost never a problem. There was magic in our lives, even then.

We fought rarely, Iris and I, and made up quickly. Iris often went with me when I went into the woods with my paper and paints, and we found that we knew each other's thoughts without a need for their being spoken aloud. Even this day, we need just a glance to convey what is in our minds, a phenomenon that has many times proved invaluable.

It was Iris who first realized my beginning love for your Uncle Harry, long before there was acknowledgement on my part. She stood with me at our wedding, and it was Iris who was there at the end, without question, without censure. What took place up-stairs as my beloved husband died becomes the basis for the pages you are reading now. In many ways, it became the basis of the rest of our lives. It was Iris who introduced the facts of Harry's death to Lily and to Daphne, and formed with them an iron circle of confidence.

Since Iris stood a foot taller than I, when we were children, she chided me by saying that 'I had to look up to her', which was true, but I absolutely hated her saying so! Today, I do so without hesitation. Iris is practical, speaks her own mind, brooks untruthfulness from no one, and is the most compassionate person I know. I love her dearly, and she loves me.

Iris grew to be a woman of stately proportions, and she married a man both half a head shorter and several pounds lighter than herself. Since the day of their wedding, Iris and Walter have never looked upon each other with less than love in their eyes. 'My Beauty', Walter calls her, and so she is. He lights up when we walk into his drug store, stops whatever he is doing, and insists on personally mixing our cherry phosphates. I will be eternally grateful that I have not been the only one to recognize the splendor that is Iris.

My husband had a great appreciation for my friend's intelligence, and encouraged the questions Iris had regarding his world of medicine. Harry taught both of us the methods of extracting essences from his various herbs and distilling them into tinctures of varying strengths. Our little bottles of mint oils, lavender and sage are the treasures of our kitchens. Others of the Doctor's herbal extracts found themselves used in remedies formulated by Iris' husband. Those that went to Walter's pharmacy shelves came from specimens grown behind the walls of Harry's private reserve. Even Walter was not permitted entry to the sacred space of my husband's herbal sanctuary, but he knew what grew there, and had full access to the special plants that were used in his remedies. Later on, I became well acquainted with the properties of those guarded plants. Oh, yes indeed, I learned. All four of us did.

Iris

Lily

Lily

A h, Lily. I have always loved the name she chose for herself, as it so pleasantly slips over the tongue when spoken. Lily's mother and my own, each of them unique for being professional women, were fast friends. It was a request put to me by my mother that began my association with Lily.

A year after the heroic death of Lily's father during the Battle of El Caney, her mother became a schoolteacher. I have figured that Lily was just shy of her ninth birthday when news arrived of her father's death during that brief and awful war. My own mother was a nurse, and her work required time spent at the school where Lily's mother taught first grade.

When I was approached with a plea for my help, Lily was just a child, as far as I was concerned. After all, I was going to high school, and Lily was only in sixth grade! Asked to befriend this child, to take her under my wing, was a task that I wanted no part of. My mother left it up to me, one of her clever devices, but told me how Lily had become more and more shy since the death of her father, and how she now preferred the comforts of her room to mixing with other people her age. Both mothers were truly concerned, and each hoped that I could help Lily to 'leave her shell and get out in the world' by including her among my friends.

Reluctantly, to say the least, I resigned myself to take Lily on as a project. As Iris and I were such constant companions, the project soon evolved into a partnership. So we dragged Lily along with us on our outings, hoping to jolly her up a bit. Once she 'came out of her shell', we thought, she would form her own friendships, and our job would be done. The sooner, the better, as far as we were concerned!

Lily, tall and slim, has an unusual face. Her eyes, wide set and gray, gaze independently from below a high forehead. I find it impossible to look into both eyes at the same time, a characteristic that both fascinates and perplexes me, as it sometimes seems there are two Lily's in there. I swear that one eye can reflect amusement while the other remains quite sober – spooky. Brows and lashes that match Lily's pale blonde hair almost disappear against her skin, further featuring the eyes that they frame. Her fair hair was fashioned that summer into long, fat curls by her mother, and tied to one side by a large satin-ribbon bow. It was the style for little girls, not someone Lily's age, but she seemed not to notice.

Despite all efforts during our summer of 'project Lily', Lily remained reclusive. Iris and I included her within our larger sphere of friendships, set up socials with girls her own age, and introduced her to our Lutheran youth group. Although she overcame her reticence to accompany us during that time and had actually relaxed and seemed to enjoy our being together, she remained quite shy and retiring. We simply came to let her be that way, to let her be Lily, and we began to relax our attitude toward her. By the time school was about to start again, Iris and I concluded that we had been pretty much a failure at rescuing our charge. We had tried and she had tried, we both agreed. Then, one morning, on the day of our last outing together before summer vacation was over, Lily surprised us. She blushingly thanked us for being her friends, and hoped that we would always be close.

"I just," she told us, "can't help it. I simply don't like most people, but," she went on as we listened intently, "I love you both and I always will, no matter what. This has been the best summer of my whole life."

With that, Lily gave each of us a tinfoil wrapped package and watched carefully as we opened them. Inside small boxes were bracelets, braided and beaded by Lily, each bearing a small, heart shaped charm. They matched the one worn by our new friend, for such she had become without our realizing it.

Over the next few years, Lily did form a few friendships, and selectively worked with our Lutheran youth group. Some people considered her aloof, while others thought her mature and dignified. We knew that she was none of these. Shyness is so often misinterpreted.

Iris and I maintained an alliance with Lily during the rest of our high school years and the beginning of hers, but began to lose contact with her after our graduations. I did not really connect with her again until after my marriage to your Uncle Harry and my return to White Laurel. By then, Lily had become a schoolteacher herself. She and her mother now worked at the same school, and continued to live in their wonderful old house. Teaching agrees with Lily, and mothers are overjoyed when their children are assigned to her classroom. So, apparently, are the children.

It was Lily's position, actually, that reintroduced her to our lives. On a day that found both Daphne and Iris working with me, Lily brought her twelve pupils for a nature study, to Norris Gardens. It was a delight to witness her work with the children, as questions were asked and answered or noted for research. The three of us found ourselves engrossed for the entire afternoon with her class of eager youngsters. Pansies were being set out that day. Daphne made sure that each child potted one to take home, and insisted that Lily have several for her classroom. Daphne had met Lily for the first time that afternoon, and was quite impressed with the relationship between her and her enthusiastic pupils, as were Iris and I.

———————

Our summer project, tall and slender in her long black skirt and mutton chop sleeved shirtwaist, had reentered our world a woman worth knowing.

The Mission

Janeylib, I need to stop here a bit to remind you of something. Do you remember the little nosegays called tussie mussies that you and I used to assemble from flowers and leaves? Do you remember my telling you of how romantic trysts could be arranged, sinister plots revealed, by deciphering their floral clues? Well, Daphne, Lily, Iris and I were intrigued with the definitions of those clues, and chose Compton's "Cyclopedia" from among many little books on the subject, as our guide to interpretation. We decided to send messages to each other in this secret way, and among us, ribbons that tied our little bouquets lent meaning also. The sender was identified by her color of ribbon, while knots in bow and streamers indicated the day of the week, and the time that was appointed for a meeting. Always, when a tussie mussie was received, one had been summoned. Tussie mussies delivered the morning that your great uncle died had been ringed with oak leaves.

———

Harry's death was to take place. We had meticulously planned it together. It was more than time. Surcease for my beloved husband, and his grateful passage from an unalterable world of pain, made our choice pure and absolute.

———

I had been taught well by my husband the methods of administering 'sweet release', as Harry termed our lethal preparations. I was a naturally curious and eager student as Harry revealed to me the properties of plants grown within the walls of his garden. My eagerness to learn methods of isolating and extracting their deadly poisons both fascinated and appalled me. It appears that your love of chemistry, Janeylib, is one that we share.

The shelves of our sun porch laboratory became stocked with roots, berries, seeds, bulbs and various other parts from the planted partners we had coaxed into growing their poisons for us. From our aerie apothecary came powders, tinctures and extracts, measured precisely for the jobs they were called upon to do. All the tender care given the Doctor's private garden was about to be repaid in kind. White plumes had crowned the camas bulbs used for Harry's departure. Extract from our foxglove's root helped to insure that his leave-taking was a swift one.

Harry and I had never been closer than on his last earthly morning. He had known for several months, before telling me, that our time together was coming to a close. His final weeks, he told me, would be continually agonizing for both of us, and he did not wish either of us to experience that kind of pain and heartbreak. I had already begun to see my husband's decline, and had vainly tried to ignore it or wish it away. Perhaps I should have tried to dissuade him, but I truly don't believe so. It was my own choice that I concoct my husband's preferred formula myself, and to be with him while he died. It was the highest act of love I have ever performed.

It turned out to be Harry who consoled me that gray winter's morning, not the other way around. Even in his last moments, before he turned inward to embrace what waited there, it was his hand that held mine. I lay with him, then across him, as he died, seeking my own stillness while his came all too soon. For a time, incapable of moving, I remained prostrate, my body shielding my lover against a force that had already departed and taken a part of my spirit as well. Feeling the totality of nothingness, willing my own death, my lone breathing deafened me. Then, after how long a time I cannot say, a barely perceptible warmth began to make itself known, seeping from some unknown ember in my soul, and my life flickered once more into being.

———

In all my days, I shall never be ready to do what I was a willing part of, on that cold, early February morning.

———

Whilst I finally descended the long dark stairs of our home as a widow that day, I found that Time had progressed without me, for the last, low rays of winter sun were framed in the landing's window. The finality of Harry's suffering both assuaged and angered me, while chill again pervaded my senses. But, there they were, all three of them, standing at the foot of the stairs. The surprising warmth of Iris' hand brought me within the space of safety formed by the presence of herself, Daphne, and Lily. As the enormity of what had just transpired upstairs swept over me, they all appeared physically larger. Garbled voices sounded from somewhere beyond me, where mouths moved and words were indistinct. Six arms reached forward to embrace me as my body lost its ability to remain upright, and I sank, thankfully, to the carpet. Not fully unconscious, I was dimly aware of being lifted to the davenport and blanketed, of soft concerned voices, of the unfamiliar vantage point of looking from below, at the faces of these three women. The exaggeration of chins and nostrils above their bent over bosoms was suddenly amusing, and I heard my own brief, ragged laughter before swooning into sleep.

———

Thus does Mother Nature grant us a cushion, a respite between the before and the forever after.

———

Iris had already known, when I had told her, of Harry's cancer. She had walked into her husband's pharmacy two months prior, and come upon Walter while he was compounding a prescription. As he turned toward her, she had seen his sweet, cherished face contorted by pain. Answering her unspoken question, Walter had turned the bottle toward his wife, showing her the label and for whom the prescription was intended. Shocked herself, Iris cocooned her husband as he sobbed into the comfort of her familiar bosom, bathing her with the universal water of grief. Her own tears had come later, she said, for Harry and for me, but mostly for her own helplessness. This was a void she could never fill. Friends since boyhood, Harry and Walter were as bonded as Iris and I.

It was Iris, who knew without my telling, what Harry and I had planned. It was Iris' arms which held me first, Iris' voice crooning softly as I sank into oblivion after Harry died.

When Mr. Jenkins came with his horse-drawn hearse for my husband's body, he entered the room to find it strewn with fragrant rosemary, and with petals from last summer's roses. Harry's body had been lovingly anointed with our oils of lavender and rosemary.

Three weeks to the day after Harry's death, snowdrops appeared above their frost-flecked mulch of oak leaves. Automatically, I bent to stroke them, and glimpsed tiny purple orbs of grape hyacinths peeping up beside them. Together, for we always are in our gardens, Harry and I went in search of other harbingers of spring. We were rewarded with more snowdrops and the promise of a crocus, before February reasserted itself with a suddenly darkened sky and morbid cold. Deep gray and swollen, cotton-batting clouds pressed ever lower to the earth with their burden. As I turned reluctantly toward the house, fat flakes were shaken loose, petaling the gardens with companions to my just-discovered early bloomers. Tilting back my head to enter this winter experience, I was awarded soft snow kisses on my cheeks and into my mouth.

As swiftly as the world about me had changed, my inner skies blackened and consumed my breath. Without warning, tears that had lain in wait behind the fortress of my eyes formed streams of salty heat over my face and neck. I keened into the wind, whose own howling was its answer to my unexpected rage. I dropped to the ground and tore at the small white blossoms that had the unmitigated gall to live, clawed blindly at unyielding frozen earth, and gulped in icy air. I lay without breathing, while snow simply kept on falling. When I finally got up and went to the kitchen door, my hair and coat were leaden with their burden of snow. As the clothing I removed fell sodden to the floor, all of my stoicism, and qualities I had considered strengths, began to crackle. Within an instant, while I watched them turn to diamond dust, they were gone - no longer useful, no longer me. I stood silently in the space left by their departure and wondered what, if anything, would take their place.

Drawing a warmed blanket around my chilled body, I folded myself around a cup of tea, sat in Harry's rocker, and witnessed the whirling wonder of white blowing just beyond my protected gaze. Gratitude slowly intruded, despite my defiant stance against it. Gratitude at first, for glass; then for window frames which held their panes; for walls supporting those frames - walls with soul breathed into them by those whom they have sheltered - for roofs, and chimneys, and for Santa Claus. Random thoughts swirled about to the tempo of the snowflakes, in one spot for only a blink, before melting, or moving on. Lulled by allowing my mind freedom to wander at will while I watched the slowing winter storm, I scarcely noticed the cooling of my tea and the passing of day. Night blended with afternoon like black coffee into dishwater.

My own life crystallized after Harry's death. Selfhood's protective cloak of ice went with me everywhere, letting me see out, but walling me in. I spent a bit of time in limbo.

Two things happened toward the end of this time, Janeylib. The first set my footsteps on a pilgrim journey leading beyond any foreseeable horizon, the accounting of which you are about to read. The second provided balance to that precarious path – the surprising inclusion of your mother's presence in my life. Matilda, as you know, is the daughter of my elder sister, and the bond formed between us that spring ultimately led to your becoming my summer companion, my love.

On the Saturday after Easter, as I was about to join the Floraphiles arriving to work winter mulches into the spring soil, a tussie mussie was delivered. Pressing a coin into the young hand of Lucas Schooner, I turned back toward the house, somewhat puzzled. Oddly, the small bouquet trailed a rainbow of purple, yellow and white, showing it to have come from all three of my comrades. By the two streamers of blue, it showed that my home was to be the meeting place. One of the blue streamers held three knots, while the bow had none. They would arrive at three that afternoon.

At only one time had all been summoned, and that was the occasion of Harry's departure. Unusual selections of leaves and flowers in this tussie-mussie sent me to my desk, where B.C. Compton was waiting to help unravel the mystery. As my curiosity became assuaged with each revelation, my concern rose in response. A small packet of allspice had been tucked among globe amaranth. I found flowering reed, phlox, and goldenrod surrounded by leaves of oak, bay, and locust. Thus were 'compassion, immortality, confidence in heaven, and precaution' encircled with 'I change but in death, affection beyond the grave', and 'bravery'.

The remainder of the morning was spent working with the Floraphiles, and I welcomed the distracting effects of physical labor. At one o'clock, we stopped work for the day, and I began preparations for my friends' arrival. After a bath and change of clothes, I set about measuring, mixing, and patting out dough for scones. Brushed with butter, dotted with bits of ginger, dusted with cinnamon sugar, and into the oven they went. Our periwinkle cups and saucers were set out on a pale blue cloth, along with matching napkins, on my kitchen table.

I had run out of things to do. Thoughts kept at bay while I was busy were no longer harnessed. Although aroma and warmth filled the space around me, the air I breathed felt cold. So, I put on a shawl, the kettle for tea, a less concerned face, and waited. Time snapped its fingers, tea was brewed, and scones were nested into their napkin lined basket. Voices and footsteps ascending the front porch steps announced the women's arrival.

As usual, Iris and Lily were a background for Daphne, who, dressed in pale yellow and green, was rival to the daffodils that were just beginning to bloom. Fully appreciative of her own good fortune, Daphne enjoyed the effect she had on others, but considered her good looks just a matter of luck. We were each of us beautiful, according to her. She was right, of course, but still, Daphne was the one we all loved to look at.

Lily and Iris also wore color that day – funny, the things we remember. Iris still sported that dull gray wrap of hers, but she had topped it with a hat strewn with roses, and they complimented her extraordinary complexion. Under the wrap that she tossed over the newel post, Iris wore a shift of lavender over a skirt of deeper purple, and her costume coaxed color from her eyes, lending their blue a touch of lilac. Lily had stepped into a dress of soft blue lawn, sashed with a deep scarlet ribbon tied in a bow at her waist. She looked like the girl from years ago, and I remarked that she should wear color more often.

The air of spring had entered with them, but my sense of chill prevailed.

Finally, as we were seated around my kitchen table with our communion cups of tea, Daphne was the first to broach the reason for this gathering of the clan.

"We have to help them, Flora. All three of us have agreed on that; we just have to do it," she blurted out her rush of words, "and you, by Grace, know how to make it look natural. You know which ones to use and how they work and how to make them and you just have to teach us so that we can help them," she said so rapidly, that it was hard to hear clearly precisely what she was saying. "Just as you helped your Harry."

That, I heard.

"Wait once, Daphne." It was Iris, tossing a stone into the stream of Daphne's words. "What Daphne is saying for the rest of us Flora, is that we, with extreme discretion of course, propose to become missionaries of mercy. We have thought and spoken of little else since Harry's death; of how brave and compassionate an act it was by each of you, to help him die. The kind of senseless suffering Harry would have known is the kind we would all like to prevent." Iris paused, gauging my initial reaction. Seeing nothing but my blank stare, she pressed forward.

"I watched my brother wither away slowly while his body was devoured by something the doctor wouldn't name and couldn't cure," Iris said. " 'Stomach complaint,' the doctor called it, since he didn't know what else to say. Long after the six weeks' prediction of his death, Arthur lingered on. You remember Arthur, Flora. He prayed for his release. We all did. By the time it eventually came we were as much angered as grieved. No one deserves to live like that. No one deserves to die like that. I have since wished, with all my heart, that I had helped him."

———

"It was my Mam's sister we took in," Daphne spoke softly and deliberately now. First they took off one of her bosoms, and for a time we thought she would be all right. Then the disease came back and she had to have the other one off. She was never going to get better, and she knew it. She just had to watch herself get weaker and weaker while the sickness and the pain got stronger and stronger. She stopped saying that it was God's will long before her end, and begged to be taken in her sleep. My Mam could not bear listening to her sister talk like that. But I listened. Mam came into her room one afternoon and found that Auntie Maude had died in her sleep, as she had wanted to, finally."

———

"Daphne, Daphne, what are you saying? What are you all asking?" I cried out, even though I was becoming alarmingly aware of the answer to my second question. "Did you do something that ended your aunt's suffering, Daphne? How old were you?"

"I held the pillow to her face until she just went limp and then held it for a long time more, to be sure. Auntie Maude knew that I was there, half smiled with lips all dry and crinkly when I sat beside her bed. She knew what I was going to do. I told her. That's why she smiled – and nodded – hadn't done anything even close to that for ever so long. I was fifteen, to answer your question about my age. I knew I'd be condemned to hell if I was found out, so I have never told a single soul until now. My Mam was just so grateful, said her sister's prayers had been answered at last. I had supposed that I might feel guilty, or remorseful, or at least sad, but that didn't happen. I just felt really at peace inside, like what I had done was truly good. I'm absolutely sure that my not telling anyone about what I had done is what saved me, although my secret sometimes screamed to get out. The only voice I had to listen to was my own, and it had nothing condemning to say.

———

Our collective silence following Daphne's revelation lent a taffy-pull stretch to Time's passage. Then, gently, Lily physically turned Daphne toward herself. Taking Daphne's head between her own long, slim fingers, she began to smooth away the aftermath of Daphne's confession. We watched transfixed, as Lily's thumbs reached up between Daphne's eyebrows, stroking with just a hint of pressure, the furrows from her forehead. Then, raising her fingers to meet their partners, she made soft, deliberate circles on Daphne's temples, extending her touch beyond, to the coppery curls behind her ears. Silent tears began to wet Daphne's cheeks, swept along their path by slowly shifting fingers as Lily moved with upward strokes along Daphne's nose and under her eyes, down to her chin, beyond to her throat. Her hands worked unhurriedly to the back of Daphne's neck and patiently massaged the base of it. Daphne's eyes had closed, and her head drooped softly forward. Lily circled once again to her throat, brushed lightly over her face, and then lowered her fingers to rest fore and middle fingertips gently in the hollow between Daphne's clavicles. This ending spot had a profound effect. Daphne abruptly cried hard for just the briefest time, and then became completely calm. Lily removed her hands by sliding them smoothly across Daphne's shoulders. Then she leaned forward, raised Daphne's face to her own, and lightly kissed her. The transformation that had taken place was beyond ordinary description. It was magic.

Since her arrival, Lily had been both observer and participant without saying a word. Since I truly expected Lily to dissent from the others, I had been waiting for her opposing view. While I poured fresh tea into our cups, replacing that which had cooled, Lily commenced to surprise me. Against the background of hush that filled the room, her voice sounded with a resonance that spelled authority.

"Flora, this is hard for you, as your experience with Harry is still a presence," Lily began. "I know that. We all do. But, there is someone who needs our help, right now, which is why we are here this afternoon. There is just no time to wait until a later date to plead our case. You remember my two aunts who live in Mauch Chunk, the midwives who have been there for what seems forever. Each of us here owes something to them. Aunt Sadie taught each of us how to use Queen Anne's lace seeds. Daphne here was terrified, after her first two, that she would have a baby every year. Thanks to Sadie, she didn't."

I listened with mounting concern to the proposal that all three of these diverse women were suggesting. If I understood correctly, they wanted to kill people. My mind played tiddlywinks. Well, wasn't this what I had so recently done? But, that was different. How was it different? It just was! It was something Harry and I had planned together. That made it different. Didn't it? The honest answer was one that I did not want to entertain. It came to me nonetheless. I began to listen with a clearer ear.

"Lily," I asked, still attempting to fathom the reason for this afternoon's assemblage, "what is bringing you into this potential disaster? You are generally the one of us least agreeable to anything that might interfere with our lives staying as they are. You are the one I seek out, for Lord's sake, when I need answers to my own questions. Please, assure me that you are sane: I need to hear this. And what is wrong with Sadie or Sophie?"

"My own story is not yet in the telling, Flora," she answered, regarding me with those clear, gray, far-apart eyes and ignoring the question of her sanity. "Aunt Sadie is fine, even though she has slowed down some of late, and Sophie is still trekking up into the Poconos to bolster her constitution, whenever she can get away long enough for a healthy hike. They are both still birthing babies, even though there is a new doctor in town. He apparently works with them sometimes, and finds it amazing that they have lost only two mothers in all their years of service. I took the train over to visit them last week and went with them on a call that turned out to be a false alarm. I had so hoped to be there for a birthing. It might be taking place right now, for all I know. No," Lily concluded, "they are still busy, being the godsends that they are."

"Well then," I asked, "what brings them into this afternoon's discussion?"

"It's Brucie."

"Brucie? Who is Brucie?"

"Brucie is the love of their lives, and he is so crippled up, he can't even get up by himself anymore. Every step he takes when they raise him is absolute agony, and now he has just about gone blind. He still eats, but very little, and howls in pain each time he rolls over," Lily said. "It breaks their hearts to watch him suffer, but even they can't do anything more to help him. For years Brucie has guarded their doors and hiked the hills with Aunt Sophie; he slept next to Sadie every night until she could walk again, after her nasty fall. They have had a love affair which most humans don't achieve among themselves, although it is not so uncommon between humans and their dogs."

"Ah," I exclaimed with relief, "so Brucie is a dog! How long have they had him?"

"Thirteen years."

"That's a good long time for a dog," said Daphne. "One of ours is almost eight, and we already dread the thought of losing her."

"This is the point I am coming to," said Lily. "These two women, who have made difficult decisions all their lives, are agonizing over what to do for Brucie. Neither one of them could 'put him down', they told me. They have cared for his needs themselves for all of his life, and having some stranger perform the deed is out of the question. After listening to them go back and forth and get nowhere, I mentioned that perhaps we might help them, that some of us knew natural ways to terminate life."

"So this whole concept was yours, Lily?" I asked incredulously. "I am astonished at this - not critical, truly, just thoroughly surprised, pleasantly, actually. What an amazing day this is turning out to be."

"As a matter of fact," Lily returned, "this whole idea rather came together for us all after Harry died. None of us then knew Daphne's story, but we knew yours, and Iris shared hers. So, in some large sense, you began this concept, as you call it, Flora. We have spoken of little else these past six weeks. Now, if you agree, our first beneficiary will be Brucie. Iris has some idea of how to proceed, but you are the one that has studied and perfected ways of creating angels. Brucie will be blessed by our ministrations and will leave this world having provided us a first experience, well, first for Iris and me, in euthanasia. Since Brucie was born a dog, which among humans is considered a lower status of life, we will not be doing anything against the law. To my mind," she concluded with a decisive nod of her head, "human beings deserve every bit as much consideration as dogs receive."

Lily reached for a scone, buttered it, and never took her eyes from my face. This had been quite a speech for the most reflective member of our group. Clearly there had been much deliberation within my circle of friends prior to their coming to me for guidance. With mixed emotions, I busied myself with another pot of tea, then decided that a splash of blackberry brandy would be just the thing to top it off. Part of me appreciated the fact that they had waited awhile after Harry's departure to approach me, but the rest of me felt excluded. So, my questions to Lily were direct, and perhaps rather blunt.

"Do Sadie and Sophie agree to our help?"

"Not only do they agree, they are hoping for us to come directly."

"Do they know that even though Brucie is a dog, he is about to become a guinea pig?"

"They do," Iris chimed in. "Flora, Daphne and I have both spoken to Aunt Sadie on the telephone. We dared not discuss why we wished to travel to see them, in case someone else was on the line, but Aunt Sadie told each of us how anxious she and Sophie are to have us for a visit. I promised that we will come soon, which we shall, whatever our decision turns out to be," she said.

"One other question to you all," I ventured. "Well, two, actually. First, do these two women have any idea how you are proposing to use this experience with Brucie on future prospects? My second question depends on how you answer this one."

"Again, Flora," Lily spoke with gathering firmness, "they do. The three of us spoke at length during the time I was with them. It was Aunt Sophie who made the suggestion, a plea, really, that Brucie be the first to benefit from our plan. It would give Brucie's life the honor it deserves, is how she put it. The sooner, the better."

Lily paused, drank from her cup, and waited a bit for comments from the others or me. Hearing none, still directing her voiced thoughts toward me, she went on.

"As far as our aiding humans is concerned," Lily resumed, "Aunt Sophie simply said 'Amen' to my proposal. Aunt Sadie firmly offered her agreement. While they warned as to the very real risks we take, and stressed extreme caution, they nevertheless blessed our undertaking. The risk factor is what makes you key to our venture, Flora. You are the one of us who knows which of Mother Nature's children carries the means of terminating life. You have the equipment, and have mastered the techniques necessary for extracting and distilling poisons from things that grow in Harry's gated garden, poisons that are not readily detected as a cause of death. We are asking you to teach us that which you have learned, so that we can do for others what you did for Harry. Responsibility will not rest squarely on your shoulders; each of us agrees to mutually share all aspects of our mission, from beginning to end. We have plenty of time to prepare thoroughly for our fellow humans, but Brucie needs us now. The four of us can take the train to Mauch Chunk in the morning, do our work, and catch the afternoon train home again, mission accomplished. If you agree to this, we would like to make the trip on Thursday, which gives us a day to observe your methods of preparation. Mother has agreed to teach my class that day. We realize that you will need time to think about our extended proposal, and we all need time to talk about it, but if you think at all kindly toward what we ask, please, help us now with Brucie."

There was a catch in her voice as Lily came to the end of her speech, and my own thoughts buzzed about like bees in a jar. Privately, I had entertained the very ideas just introduced. I had also envisioned discovery and its consequences. The fact that Sophie and Sadie already knew of this possible venture disturbed me. As a widow without dependents, I was responsible only to myself, but Iris and Daphne had prominent husbands. Along with that, Daphne had three children to consider, and Lily held a respected teaching position. So, my second set of questions centered on these concerns.

"How do you propose keeping this plan of yours from becoming known?" I asked. "Sadie and Sophie already know of it. How can you be certain that they would not reveal, at some point in time, the things you have told them? Have you truly considered the repercussions to your family, Daphne, to James, of all people, his being a lawyer? And you, Iris. Walter is highly respected as a druggist, and many people know of his long friendship with Harry. Dear God, don't these things concern you?"

"Who do you think taught Harry all he needed to know, Flora, of how to produce from his plants the toxins he needed?" Iris retorted quickly. "Harry didn't gain that knowledge on his own."

"Great Guns, Iris," I shot back. "This is just one shock after another this afternoon. I never even considered how Harry learned to do what we did in the laboratory. I supposed that he got it all from his medical training."

"Extracting, distilling, compounding, required dosage, these are the skills of a pharmacist," Iris, her forehead furrowed, went on. "I know a little about these things, but this is Walter's world, and he taught Harry. Harry taught you, Flora, and now we ask you to teach us. I find no reason for Walter's knowing anything of what, hopefully, we will be doing. If my husband suspects," she declared, "I will deal with it."

Lily told me that, in regard to her aunts' trustworthiness, she had no doubts. They had, during their years as midwives, made questionable decisions of their own.

————

The three faces watching my own had been known to me for years. As I returned their gazes, I found each one subtly altered. I was never again to see them as they had been before this day.

I drained the tea from my cup, added a healthy splash of brandy, and sat apart from the others, in Harry's rocker. The seat warmed beneath me while the brandy took the chill from my brain. Harry felt less close to me than was usual when I sat in his chair. He had been becoming more distant by degrees. My decision was to be a solitary one.

"Brucie will be aided," I said finally to my three waiting companions. "It will take some time for me to think about the rest."

They nodded in unison, which struck me as comical. I laughed, and Time snapped to attention. We chatted about other things and the afternoon went on. But, a corner had been turned. Our work had begun, and we absorbed the finality of that, each in her own way.

The Passengers—
Ticket Number One

The next day dawned in glory. Slanted rays of early sun shone boldly through my lace curtained windows, creating shifting patterns of light on the wallpaper. I stretched deliciously between still-warm sheets, sleepily unaware in those first few moments of day of anything other than its bright beginning. Short lived as those moments were, they remain fixed in my mind as an overture to the life-altering symphony about to receive its downbeat. When thoughts of our venture flowed into my mind, there was no more room for reflection. My day had begun. Some days never really end, do they, Janeylib?

Daphne, Lily, and Iris arrived together, dressed for working in the garden; since this was not a scheduled day for volunteers, the four of us were quite alone. It was early in the year for most of the plants about which they were to learn to be in bloom, but our darling hellebores nodded their flowering heads in greeting. Purples, whites, and my favorite pale greens bobbed in the morning breezes. "These sweet lovelies can kill," I told my sober audience. This was the first of many such revelations, and the beginning of our irreversible undertaking. "All parts of hellebores are toxic," I went on, "roots and rhizomes especially so. They affect the heart and ability to draw breath. Their powders have been in common use for years to kill lice and caterpillars. I already have a supply of hellebore parts, so we will not need to harvest any today. Follow me upstairs to the sun porch, and we will decide how best to help poor Brucie."

Only the tread of footfall behind, as I entered the house and ascended the stairs, assured me that they were following.

The volume of their silence echoed in the hallway as we approached the sunroom's locked door. It was the first I had entered our laboratory since Harry's death, and the bright morning sun made dazzling jewels of our variously filled glass jars and our equipment. I instantly remembered how Harry had needed to lead me from this room and down the stairs after we had taken what we needed for his demise, the stronger of us, even then. Now, bright daylight interrupted my brief reverie and illuminated new faces. Our work was about to be resurrected.

"We don't have the time today," I emerged from drifted thoughts, "to begin a totally new preparation for Brucie. Ideally, we should visit our beneficiary before we administer the dose. We need to determine physical states - his weight and ability to swallow, along with the advancement of disease, are of prime importance. I do have a compound of white plumed camas and hellebore on hand. It will need to be substantially reduced in strength for Brucie, which we will do with distilled water. Is he able to eat or drink?" I asked Lily.

"He barely eats, no matter what Sophie coaxes him with. He does better with taking water, but even that seems to gag him sometimes," she answered.

"Well then," I told them, "what we need to do is to prepare some suppositories, just in case, by combining powders with cocoa butter. No raised eyebrows. That was a surprise. "Anyone unfamiliar with their administration?"

"Never did it, never want to," was Lily's immediate reply. "I won't say 'never would', but I would really rather not have to be the one."

"I felt that same way, Lily," Iris spoke quietly. "It's amazing what I found myself doing for Arthur when his stomach couldn't hold onto anything and the pain got so bad. You won't have to do the suppositories, Lily, if you don't want to. We will all find parts of what we will be doing distasteful, I am sure."

Iris was the one among us, other than myself, who was

familiar with the use of scales and measurements. All were solemn students that afternoon, and quick ones, as lessons leading to an uncertain future began. For the final time I questioned them about their determination to proceed. I was assured that, despite some strong pulls to the contrary, this decision was firmly secured. Individually and as a circle, we were prepared to move ahead. I did not learn until much later the soul searching that preceded my friends' commitment. To my mind, there was more to be lost by our pretty Daphne than by the rest of us; yet, here she was, determined and dedicated as all of us were to carry onward despite the very real risks we were taking. She later confided that this was only the second big decision she had made on her own since marrying James. 'Heady wine,' she described her doing so. Heady, indeed. Our Daphne was proving to be a great deal more than simply confection for the eye.

We met at the Lehigh Valley station to board the Thursday morning train, four friends off to pay a social call on the midwives of Mauch Chunk. Two hours and fifteen minutes later we were in the company of two already-grieving women and one incurable, miserable dog. Little time was given to greeting. It was work we had come to do. We behaved, I must say, quite professionally.

Brucie sensed our presence and, I think, our reason for being there. His clouded eyes spoke his need to our hearts and rendered the permission we needed. Lily laundered her hands in the basin provided by Sophie, then knelt beside Brucie. She placed his head on her lap, kissed the spot above his eyes, and spoke words that only the two of them could hear. Brucie whimpered softly, and Lily extended her palm. I poured into it the elixir formulated the day before. Offering his escape to Brucie, Lily sang softly to him while he put out his tongue and managed to lap the liquid from her hand.

It was all over so quickly that it seemed not to have happened at all. We stood for a few moments, each of us engrossed in her own way, while the finality of the beginning of our mission pulsed within my every heartbeat. Again Lily's hands were bathed, and the remnants of Brucie's final kiss were washed away.

Sophie wrapped his worn blanket up and around the form that had contained her much loved friend. Together, she and Sadie lifted the still warm animal and carried him to his favorite spot beneath the sweet gum tree, where the place prepared for him was waiting. The sun sent dappled beams between leftover leaves. Cardinals and mockingbirds formed a choir in the highest branches. The two sisters who were Brucie's mothers spoke of his life and of their lives together. They placed alongside him his old rubber ball and the collar he'd not worn for months. Each of us added those things we had been given for the occasion - a small framed photograph of the three companions, a whistle no longer to be blown, a fragment from his food dish, a worn shoe that bore marks of his puppy teeth. Then the two older women left us and returned to their house, while we four covered Brucie's bones with the soil in which he had buried so many.

Our return to White Laurel that afternoon was spent in companionable quiet. The clickety-click of wheels on track was a lullaby to me, and I dozed a good part of the way home. Iris had brought along her knitting bag, and her needles made their own soft clicking as she worked. Lily and Daphne spoke softly to each other on occasion, but mostly they gazed outward, at the Pennsylvania trees speeding past.

The Passengers - Ticket Number One

Prelude

Prelude

The next several weeks brought spring back to our part of the world. On most days there were Floraphiles working in the gardens, and I often joined them. The Doctor's walled garden was one I had tended alone since his death, and it felt good to see returning shoots beside their evergreen neighbors. Several of our herbs and roots gifted us even in the dead of winter.

Daphne, Iris, Lily and I had for several years gathered on Thursday afternoons for a game of whist, a time period that had now transformed into lessons in the laboratory. I began teaching them what I had learned of white plumed camas, black-berried nightshade, and dark purple monkshood, of castor beans, and foxglove, and hellebores. Darlings of the gardens released their deeper secrets one by one to women who would tenaciously guard their knowledge of them. Autumn crocus, but not its spring cousin; all parts of the yew, except for its bright red berries; the time of year best to harvest, and specimens that were effective when dried and those needing to be fresh; all the things I had discovered with Harry, I taught them. They learned which plants gave the kinder toxins, those that quickly affected the heart and lungs, and of the nasty ones containing cyanide, that killed more painfully. We had no use for the latter, but our study included them.

On Saturdays, we often roamed the woods and marshes. Several of our most deadly plants live their lives in the wild. We discovered low, wet places where false hellebores dwell, and found the hidey-holes of water hemlock, whose roots were given up to us. Once again I marveled at the protection plan of our fellow life form, for the very toxins that kill animal life assure these plants' survival in the wild.

Underlying our efforts spent in discovery and acquisition of skills was the knowledge that we would someday be called upon to use them. Our only passenger on the train to Glory had been a dog. The specter of delivering a fellow human was laden with not only the picture of the deed itself, but also of its consequences should we be discovered. However, for a while, before it all truly began, we spent our time in the luxury of learning new facts, unfamiliar skills, and more deeply about each other

———

We termed our act of deliverance 'assisticide'. Those who received the benefits of our mission we knew as our passengers, released from this world to travel onward. Brucie was the first to receive a ticket for the train to Glory.

Neither Daphne's aunt nor my dear Harry was included on our passenger list, as they left before our combined mission began. Their deaths, however, most assuredly paved the pathway onto which we stepped.

These people about whom you will learn, Janeylib, each and every one of them, were deeply loved. Living, for those we aided, had become absolute, irreversible torment as pain and exhaustion drained away whatever flows of energy there had been within them. Methods by which they dealt with their own desperate situations varied, despite recurring themes, but each passenger, beyond question, unwaveringly wished to travel on and leave his or her body behind.

Never once did any of us seek out those we aided. More often than not we simply visited and consoled people involved in the natural process of dying, without any interference on our part. But cries for help were not ignored.

Prelude

Ticket Number Two

Our first human passenger was Millie Harper's mother. For as long as I could remember, Mrs. Harper had been said to be an old, old woman, a bony frame tucked about with quilts, as she sat staring at things beyond her vision. She had taken to her bed after the temperance train wreck at Mud Run, and had never again set foot from her door after the deaths of her men. Both of her boys were on that sixth train with their father, sitting in the last car, when the seventh temperance train plowed into theirs. All three were killed on impact, their lives over in an instant. For Mrs. Harper, who had somehow convinced them to attend the total abstinence meeting in Hazelton, life drained drop by drop.

Millie, the only Harper daughter, had some time ago escaped her family's household to become governess to three little girls in Scranton. This cherished pocket of time in Millie's life snapped shut when those two trains collided. Her mother's total withdrawal from life required Millie's return to White Laurel, and her years of familial bondage ensued. While railroad pensions ironically sustained them, Millie, seldom seen, melted into the surroundings to which she had returned. More lives than the counted dead were lost in the Mud Run wreck. The Harper house had gradually receded over time, as branches and grasses enrobed and canopied its form, further diminishing the two women held within its frame. Now, although I scarcely knew her, one of those women had sent a request to pay me a call.

Mildred Harper, when she arrived, set me aback. Ramrod straight she stood at my door, as if daring me to allow her entrance. Dressed as I imagined she was when a governess, high black shoes buttoned to the top, and ankle length dress of soft gray wool with a collar underlined by a straight, black ribbon tie. Millie had arrived exactly on time. Her hair, not yet gray, was held from her face by two large tortoise-shell combs which marginally did the job of containing the thick braids worn across her head. But Millie's cheeks were pink, and her coloring plus a slight tremor to her chin belied the mask she presented. One cheek bore a thin scar. Her eyes, pale blue mirrors, revealed nothing; they simply reflected back the curiosities they encountered. I stood to one side and held the door open for her to enter, then led her to the parlor where a pot of minted tea awaited pouring. Millie looked around the room. Then, as if satisfied with what she saw, she settled herself into the Morris chair. After receiving the offered cup with long, graceful fingers, and in a voice that was surprisingly childlike, Millie began her appeal for assistance.

"My mother has lingered for years," she began directly, "appearing to be an invalid. For much of the time, this has actually been the case. There have been periods, however, that an incongruous strength has belied her frail body and bottled fury has flung itself at what or who was in its path. Once spent, Mother's anger has receded into its unfortunate host to lay in wait, as she shriveled back to her unknowing state."

"Long ago, I learned to anticipate my mother's outbursts," Millie said. "In the beginning, I found them terrifying, as I could be the target of her rage."

"Your scar?" I asked.

"Yes, that was a welcome home gift," Millie said as she lightly stroked her cheek. "I never did sustain another one. I learned to simply leave the room when I sensed an impending tirade, and let inanimate objects receive her wrath. As the youngest child, and only girl, my leaving home at fifteen was a disaster as far as my mother was concerned. I had been well trained in assuming household duties, and Mother saw my departure as the escape she was incapable of making."

Millie paused, and then said slowly, "The deaths of my father and brothers were physical ones. Mother's, and in a sense
mine, have been more of the soul."

For a few minutes, she sat contemplating her teacup while
I adjusted myself to her presence. Millie's asking permission to
visit, in the first place, had been unanticipated. Her revelation
just now required some digestion. Finally, I gave voice to my
curiosity by telling Millie that I understood and empathized
with her challenging situation, then followed with asking,
"What brings you here to me now? Is there some way in which
you think that I could be of assistance to you?"

"Mother is breaking down, Flora, literally," Millie said,
placing her cup on its saucer. "Her bones give way with no
warning now, making her truly confined to her chair or her bed.
There is no way of restoring her to any kind of health. Even in
her absent mental state, her pain is quite evident, and her cries
against it are heartbreaking. Now, the adversary is taking over;
her railings against her torment are becoming constant. Still,
her heart continues to sustain her."

I contemplated my guest for a moment before speaking,
becoming attuned to her unwavering determination. "I am so
sorry, Millie," I told her. "This must be a truly difficult time for
you both. But, I am still curious as to how you decided to come
to me with your tale. Is there some way in which you think I
could possibly be of help?"

She replied with one word, "Harry."

"Harry?"

"Harry," Millie repeated.

"What on earth could Harry have to do with any of this?",
I thrust at her while rising from my chair and turning away.
My husband's name hung in the air, giving weight to the space
into which it had been spoken. Instinctively I reached out to
touch, felt warmth within the sudden chill of the room, and
stepped into it. I turned again to face my guest, and waited for

her answer.

"Harry was a friend, Flora," she replied in a less disciplined tone, "for years to my late brothers and, following the Mud Run wreck, to me. I knew of his love for you long before you did, and confess that I lamented it. I dared to embolden myself once, to tell Harry of my feelings for him, and Harry told me then of his heart's direction. After that incident, no more was said. Fortunately for me, our friendship remained over the years, resulting in his professional visits to my mother. These were the only times that we saw each other, and his ministrations to my mother were invaluable. As I was standing at her doorway during one of Harry's visits, I was startled to hear my mother beg him for release from her increasing torment. His response, after he motioned me to enter her room, was that it was not yet appropriate to contemplate such a request, but that when he felt the day had come, they would speak again. I could hardly believe my ears, but Harry took me aside and spelled out the torturous time that my mother's future ensured. He then taught me how to best care for her, how to cope with her violent changes in temperament, and what to look for in her decline. When the time came, he said, as it now surely has, and if he were no longer here, I was to come to you. He suspected that her heart might remain beating, which it has, while the rest of her crumbled, and that this was something you would need to know."

"So, I now seek your intercession," Millie said softly with downcast eyes, "and pray that you will grant it. I have made a hugely difficult decision in coming here this afternoon, and soon I must return home. Leaving my mother unattended is something I rarely do, even though she cannot move from the position in which she is placed. I must get back to her, but I brought with me a note from your late husband, which he asked me to deliver if this time came," and she reached into her bag.

I sat stupefied. Hearing of Millie's friendship with my husband had rattled me, and learning of his faith in my ability to aid her, his actually suggesting to Millie that I do so, both honored and angered me. I took the proffered envelope from her hand, got up from my chair and went to my kitchen to read it.

Once there, I sat down hard on the bench beside my kitchen table. Shaken by Millie's revelation, I slipped Harry's note from its sealed casing and read my husband's words.

My Love,

If you are reading this, it means that Mildred Harper has come to you as I advised. I have great confidence in your abilities should you decide to help her, but that decision must be yours alone. I occasionally found, during my many years of practicing medicine, that terminating a patient's torment was the kindest thing to do. But I had the protection of the physician's cloak. You do not.

That being said, the case of Mrs. Harper is a truly tragic one. If Mildred has come to you, believe me, her mother is more than ready to leave the world you know for the world to come. Should my relationship with Mildred concern you, banish all thoughts of an assignation between us. I waited my whole life for you.

My passing has not diminished my love for you. I wish you a long life and a happy one, my dear, dear Flora.

Yours forever,
Harry

If ever I had wished for Harry's blessing regarding the mission that Iris, Daphne, Lily and I had agreed to embark upon, it could not have arrived at a better time. The first appeal for assisticide had been made. The treacherous road onto which the four of us had agreed to travel awaited our footfall.

I returned to face my guest, and found that I had no words to express my jumbled thoughts. I could but stand and gaze uncomfortably in her direction.

Millie, respectful of my silence, leaned in toward the table for support as she rose to leave . Regaining her stature, she purposely squared her shoulders, but her eyes would not return to the hardness I had seen. Gray-blue and softened, they fluttered like a captured bird's wings, as they looked beseechingly into my own.

"I will need two days to prepare, Millie," I heard myself say, astounded by my own impulsiveness, but determined nonetheless, "and I shall be with you on the morning of the third." Tucking her arm in mine, I walked with her through my hallway, to the front door.

On hearing my reply, Millie's entire body relaxed its rigid stance and sank against my own. I was afraid that she had swooned, but she instantly recovered herself.

Mildred Harper's face, when she turned toward me, revealed a trace of a smile, as her lips caught salty drops from their limpid pools of blue.

———

Three tussie mussies ringed with oak and rhododendron leaves, then tied with trailing blue ribbon, were hastily assembled. Lucas Schooner was summoned, and he sped off on his bicycle to deliver them.

Always, I have been intrigued, and sometimes puzzled, by my own responses to life's challenges. Now, as I awaited replies from three women I thought I had known for most of my life, I experienced a sense of beginning combined with end - the sort that comes just before a major change, such as birth following a prolonged pregnancy must feel for both mother and child. Despite trepidation, and possible catastrophic changes to my life, the time had arrived. Oddly, I thought, I felt relative calm. For Daphne and me, the edge of assisticide had been dulled through our aids to aunt and husband, but for Lily and Iris, it was sharp and new.

Lily and Iris, as it turned out, were the ones to go with me on our first intercession.

———

We met the following morning in my kitchen, ready for a pot of coffee and gingerbread, not fully ready for whatever lay ahead after they had been consumed. Three solemn faces listened to my tale of Millie's visit and request. Three solid nods of affirmation followed my questioning as to whether Millie's mother should be our second passenger. They never learned of my personal assurance to Millie. We had unanimously agreed that none of us would act alone, and I breathed a huge inner sigh of relief.

A formula was decided upon for Mrs. Harper's ticket and we set to work on the distillation process. Sunlight that morning was filtered by low lying clouds, lending the laboratory a gentle glow, softening our act of decocting poisons. For awhile we concentrated on our individual tasks, each of us engrossed by her own thoughts. At one point, while pulverizing castor beans, Daphne asked just what it was that prompted Millie's coming to me. Still not completely comfortable with my own thoughts regarding my husband's connections to Millie, I had hesitated telling them the details of Millie's request. In spite of myself and my faith in Harry, there were still pictures in my mind's eye of seeing the two of them together. I chided myself for having suspicions regarding my dear Harry. In short, I was in a bit of a muddle and, I was surprised to realize, more than a bit jealous.

As it turned out, when I did explain Millie's visit and my misgivings regarding her surely innocent involvement with Harry, a volley of similar experiences was released from both Iris and Daphne. 'Best to leave the past with the past' was their consensus. I assured them that I would try to do just that, and preparation of Mrs. Harper's release received our full attention.

We had agreed, after our mission with Brucie, that performing assisticide was not something that all four of us should commonly do together, nor should the same two of us deliver passengers to the train of what we hoped was Glory on successive trips. We could all attend the funerals of course. That was to be expected. But the performance of the acts responsible for those funerals needed unassailable protection.

Since Daphne had planned to visit James' parents with her children on the appointed day, it worked perfectly well that Iris, Lily and I would pay a call to Mildred and Mrs. Harper. Iris and Lily both wished to go the following day, rather than wait. However, I had given Millie two days as well, to prepare for our visit.

So, we waited.

That third morning found the three of us gathered in the laboratory, placing vials of poison and oleander honey into an embroidered reticule. Into a second purse went candles, a small Bible, and rose petals.

The distance to Millie's home was over a mile from my door, which we accomplished on feet that walked mechanically, while our minds tried to settle themselves. If we were to turn back, this was our final chance to do so. We walked on. Time was gentle with us, and before we were fully aware of it, we had arrived. Set some distance from the road, the Harper house shrank back as we approached, for a jungle of blackberries, wisteria vines, and immensely tall grasses shielded its face.

Horse chestnut trees, magnificent in size, waggled their huge, five fingered leaves in warning, or welcome. Carefully tended marigolds surprisingly bordered the cracked cement sidewalk, while pruned and composted bushes of blooming roses flanked the path to the front steps.

"Millie's link to the land," I murmured on seeing them as we deliberately passed them by, before we slowed our step and bravely climbed the seven steps to the porch.

Millie opened her door even before we had a chance to turn the bell key. After politely greeting each of us in turn, and meeting Lily for the first time, she led us through her tessellated foyer into a large, open living room. There, as one, we paused in our tracks, and gasped. Painted onto every surface available in this room, wherever we looked, all around us, were birds. Up, up onto the high ceiling, down onto the walls of their walnut wainscoted woodlands, they swooped and soared, singing out their silent calls to each other. With clouds above them, grass and lake below, all around them a blue, blue sky, they appeared in perpetual flight, activity or repose. Saucy kingfishers, perched on telephone wires, looked like rowdy choirboys. Red headed, pileated, red and yellow bellied, and my favorite little downy woodpeckers all had found their perfect decaying trees. Cedar waxwings weighted holly branches while they gorged on the bright red berries, and nuthatches skittered headfirst down the white trunks of birch trees. Robins and rufous-sided towhees hopped on leaf-strewn ground, listening for telltale signs of a tasty worm. High overhead, in the shape of a V, flew a gaggle of wild geese, perhaps on their way to the lake painted for them on the floor below. Nests appeared here and there among branches and grasses; hanging oriole nests, wee, half tennis-ball sized hummingbird nests, and blue-egged abodes of robins. It was breath-taking! Faces of five fat baby barn swallows crowded the edge of their mud caked nest, while the enormous aerie of an eagle pair, fierce with their yellow eyes, took up an entire upper corner of the room. 'Incredulous' is the word that most closely describes my reaction on seeing this wonder. The colors, the motion, the total aliveness of this amazing space in which we stood, transformed it from a room to a hallowed hall. I, myself, am rightly considered a portrayer of nature. This work far outshone any I had ever seen.

"Millie," Iris breathed, as her eyes swept the room and came to rest at last on our hostess, "did you do all this?"

Millie, who had been studying us, simply nodded, flushed with the impact that her work had had upon us. We stood in awe, looking from the artist to her work and back again. Then, with the promise that we might return with Daphne, and spend all the time we liked among the birds of Millie's woods and heavens, we turned to the purpose of today's visit.

Millie led us all too quickly through a dimly lighted hall-way where owls were silhouetted against trees and a waxing moon. They swept silently beside us as we walked, searching for prey that would forever elude them. Curious, hooded eyes solemnly observed the progress of our short procession. We had mixed feelings about that hallway. Iris later remarked that she could have lingered there for hours, while Lily was grateful to have passed quickly through. My own interest lay in the execution of paint and brush. Millie appeared to be far more gifted than anyone under whom I had studied.

In those moments of awe, each of us had lost touch with our reason for being in Millie's home that day. We had now arrived at the doorway through which our first human passenger lay, waiting for her ticket to be delivered, and our purpose came rushing back with staggering force. Millie knocked politely, and then held the door aside for us to precede her. Each of our lives was about to be altered forever, yet we resolutely stepped as one toward Mrs. Harper's deliverance, and our own possible catastrophe.

Mrs. Harper's bedroom, almost in contrast to the room we had just seen, was painted simply. Nothing could have been more lovely for a person ailing in body and mind. Walls had been brushed with the softest blue. Stratus and cumulus clouds lifted one's eye toward a ceiling tinted an even lighter shade of the same azure color. In one corner, a sweeping rainbow faded into oblivion. An occasional pair of gulls suggested sand and sea, but only the idea of ocean was apparent. My immediate thought was that I would hate to leave such a space. One look at Mrs. Harper showed that she had, in most respects, been gone for some time.

Lily, Iris and I stepped together onto the road that proved to have no end.

Millie spoke softly to her mother, explaining our presence, and introduced each of us by name. Mrs. Harper's clouded eyes lit briefly as she rasped a word or two to her daughter. Millie then tenderly wrapped her mother's delicate body in a final embrace, turned her head and nodded to us. Iris mixed into herbal honey the product of our labors, and Millie extended her tear-moistened palm. It was not the last time we would watch the refusal of a spoon for the cup of a loving hand. Millie's mother licked the sweetness from her daughter's palm, smiled with cleared countenance into Millie's face, clouded again, and died. Her final words to her daughter had been 'thank you.'

———

Numbly flooded with emotion, I somehow lighted the candles that Iris had placed about the room. Lily sprinkled lavender water and Iris sprinkled rose, as we made our way back through the gallery of owls. Pausing briefly in Millie's magnificent aviary, we quickly crossed the patterned floor of her foyer, and stepped again into the light of day.

We all looked up, as if startled by the light, or what had just transpired. Or perhaps we were trying to catch a glimpse of the train that was now transporting a whole Mrs. Harper toward her particular Glory.

Doctor Ramsey concluded that Mrs. Harper had died peacefully in her sleep, probably of heart failure. So she had.

———

For myself, the immediate aftermath of our first assisticide for a human being was peculiarly devoid of feeling. I had expected some sort of internal response, but experienced only a sense of calm. It was not until the following morning, in those barely-conscious moments before wakefulness, that the enormity of our undertaking stood naked before me. A hot bath did little to rescue my body from its uncontrollable shivering.

Daphne, along with the three of us, attended Mrs. Harper's funeral, and met Millie for the first time. Both Iris and Daphne had persuaded their husbands to join us that morning, and a few elderly people from Mrs. Harper's past completed our small group. Walter and James, after expressing their sympathies to Millie, departed quickly following the brief service. Oddly, or perhaps not so oddly, we were the only ones to accompany Millie and her mother to the cemetery. The parson was there of course, with his words of redemption for those who believed, but he had never actually met Mrs. Harper, and he left directly after her interment, with a reminder to Millie that she should attend his Sunday services.

After the parson left, assured that we were quite alone, Millie opened the neck of an embroidered drawstring bag she had carried. She extracted from it a handful of soil, tossed it into the grave, and passed the bag for each of us to do the same. Then she emptied the bag of its remaining contents and dropped the pretty thing into her mother's grave.

"From under the horse chestnut tree," she explained of the bits of earth, "where we all used to swing, even Isobel. Isobel Irene is my mother's name, and it needs speaking aloud. It needs to rise to the heavens so that she can hear it," and she called, followed by each our voices, Isobel Irene's name into the dampening air.

Isobel Irene's casket, painted white, was child-size, so tiny had she become. Blooming fully into shades of pale then deepest pink, rosebuds that would far outlast any found in nature climbed from the underside of the coffin to crown around its head. Daphne was seeing Millie's work for the first time, and all that we had described to her paled alongside her actually seeing the scope of Mildred Harper's talent.

"Oh, Millie," she exclaimed reverently, "how truly, truly beautiful. How wonderfully you have brought to life the blossoms surrounding your mother."

Daphne was afraid, she later confided, that her remarks had not been appropriate, but they were exactly the words Millie had needed to hear.

Millie politely refused our offer that day to sit with her. She was physically alone for the first time in her life, she told us, and felt the need to experience that kind of solitude. She would be perfectly fine. We doubted her wisdom and implored her to call upon any or all of us, should she feel the slightest need. She had done that, she replied, on two occasions. She and Isobel Irene would be forever grateful.

Ten days later each of us received a bouquet of Millie's garden roses, along with an invitation to luncheon on the following Wednesday. Lily's schedule would not allow her to attend, but the rest of us cleared conflicts from our calendars. Ideas of hostess gifts were considered, discarded, and considered again. In the end, we decided to give Millie a copy of Compton's Cyclopedia along with our offer to aid in establishing a garden of her own. Thus began friendships unimagined but a short time ago. Our first foray onto the road of assisticide had fortunately been made without disclosure or discovery, much to our immense relief. It was a dangerous path we had chosen to travel, and we knew it. Committed as we were, the fears we each harbored were well grounded.

Decoration Day

Decoration Day

Spring came early the following year. Bulbs planted around the red maple bloomed and were spent before Easter, and our town became perfumed by an abundance of lilac blooms, a fragrance I wished I could trap in a jar and let out bit by bit in January. For just a bit of time, reminders of assisticide retreated from the centers of our minds.

It was Decoration Day, and we gathered together with other friends on Lily's vast front porch to drink lemonade, eat fried chicken and savor Lily's mother's star-shaped sugar cookies, while we cheered the parade going by. This was one glorious sun-blessed morning. No war was presently going on and celebration for that fact alone made our time together precious. Anna and her friends, with their red, white, and blue decorated wagons and bicycles, were all lined up, waiting for their signal to join the marchers. What a lovely young lady Anna was becoming, I thought, and said so to Lily, who quickly agreed. Anna was actually the daughter of a Polish domestic hired years ago who, after giving birth to a baby girl, left her child in the care of Lily's mother one day, boarded a ship for Poland, and never returned. Lucky Anna, we all agreed, to have been left with a loving pair such as Lily and her mother. Lily steadfastly maintains that she and her mother are the lucky ones.

Off the young folks went, into the parade, with Anna and her best friend in the lead. All had loaded branches of lilac and forsythia into their wagons and bicycle baskets, and some had woven colored ribbons through the spokes of their bicycle wheels. How full of life and colorful they were, as they followed along behind the marching war veterans!

The parade always marched to the war memorial statue in the park, where we gathered to stand at attention or with bowed heads as the names of White Laurel's fallen heroes were called one by one. We always held Lily's hands as the name of her father sounded in the air. Lily, Iris and I then walked to the graveyard to decorate his and other graves with more flowers, and ended our day with a box social on the courthouse lawn.

There was always music from the grandstand, and sometimes we saw fireworks, while the skies darkened and stars came out. I loved Decoration Day, Janeylib. You were here with me once, as I recall.

Decoration Day

Ticket Number Three

Old Mr. Lassiter was living outside of town, with his colony of cats, on the farm he had worked all of his adult life, and where he had lived since he was born. Everyone else associated with the old Schultz farm had passed on, and no one knew who really owned it anymore. It never had been much of a farm anyway, but was enough of one to sustain the people who worked it. When the cantankerous Oscar Schultz had died after breaking his neck in a fall from the hayloft, Mr. Lassiter, the hired hand, finally moved himself up to the farmhouse. Folks around town had laughingly gossiped to one another that now, he really was a handyman. Word was that Ina Schultz and Mr. Lassiter had for years been the ones to really work the farm, that her husband had just run it, and his wife, almost into the ground. Be that as it may, after her husband died, Ina began to find ways to improve the farm, managed it herself with Lassiter's help, and outlived old Oscar by a good thirty years. Ina sold some back acreage and acquired a trip of Nubian goats that she milked, and learned to make wonderful cheese. She and Mr. Lassiter became devoted to these animals and quickly established a loyal and appreciative clientele, selling their hand-made cheeses along with bottles of rich goat milk. Vernon Lassiter, it turned out, was a natural with husbandry. It was a good thing that their farm was well away from town, for the number of goats increased, along with their goat habits and smells, but they significantly enriched the lives of Ina Schultz and Vernon Lassiter.

For some time now, it had been only an ailing Mr. Lassiter and his cats living on the place. He never did regain himself after Ina's death, just stayed where they had been together, and he gradually returned to his former existence. All of the unsold goats had ultimately become neglected, and finally wandered off in search of better homes. Lassiter became a true recluse, and now angrily chased away anyone who deigned to look in on him, so folks left him alone. Most thought he hadn't a friend in the world, but he did have one. Lily.

As a child, Lily was not able to stomach milk from cows, so goat's milk had been purchased for her from the Schultz farm. During her visits to the farm, first with her mother and then on her own, Lily had found herself drawn into the easy comfort of the farmhouse and its occupants. Mr. Lassiter never missed the coal-scuttle when he spat tobacco juice, Lily told us, which fascinated her. And Mrs. Schultz didn't object to his spitting, which amazed her. Together, the couple became the weft of Lily's childhood, and they wove her into the fabric of their lives. Mr. Lassiter even made for Lily her very own rocking chair, to match his and Ina's, and carved her name, his, and Lily's date of birth into the underside of the seat. He was the daddy she had not known, and Ina Schultz, childless herself, was Lily's beloved second mother.

All of this, Lily told us one lazy August afternoon on her front porch, where we sat together chatting and stringing pole beans for canning. Anna sat with us for a bit, then jumped up and left us to join her friends. Iris conversationally asked after Lily's mother, and then remarked on how grown up Anna was becoming.

"She has become the light of my life," was Lily's reply. She reflected on this for a moment, before bringing herself to focus once again on Mr. Lassiter, and then continued speaking of him.

"Long ago, when Ina was so desperately ill, I made a promise to this dear father of mine. I swore that I would never let him suffer the way that Ina had done." Lily paused for a moment, waiting for her memories to clear.

"Vernon usually doesn't know who I am, at this point," she continued, "although he does still allow my entry into the house. I truly fear the day when he will no longer admit me. Vernon Lassiter may be hidden somewhere within the dwindling shell of his body, or perhaps he has already departed this world and is waiting for whatever is left of him to catch up. All I know for certain is that he is horribly, horribly frightened. This constant fear, and his being unable or unwilling to nourish what is left of his body, makes his days and nights interminably bleak. My daily visits are to a vacant man.

Vernon has been waiting at the station far, far too long, and I need to help him board the train. I don't ask any of you to join me in this, other than to guide me in the preparation of his ticket. This is a duty I have expected to perform for some time," Lily said, "long before we began our mission."

For several moments there was just the sound of bees in the wisteria, their sated droning hanging heavy in the air. My palms moistened as thoughts of another assisticide loomed, and I silently considered Lily's appeal for assistance.

After a bit, Daphne interrupted the bees' industrious humming. "It sounds as if you have already made a decision, Lily, one which I personally think merits our help," she said in assurance, and the rest of us nodded. "I, for one," she went on, "will gladly go with you to the farm. You may find yourself grateful for a loving shoulder after your friend sets forth on his journey. If it will help, I can arrive a little later, after a time you feel that Mr. Lassiter will have left this world completely behind."

Lily reached across her green wicker table to take Daphne's freckled hand in hers. It wasn't the first time she had seen Daphne's depth of sensitivity.

"Dear, dear Daphne," she replied, gazing with both her eyes into Daphne's concerned face, "I so admire your insight, and appreciate your offer more than I can say, but I feel that I must accomplish this on my own. I expect that I will stay for some time within the walls of that house, after this beloved man has left it. It will be harder for me to say goodbye to all that is within that house than it will be for me to assist Vernon Lassiter."

"Have you considered, Lily, how it might seem to some unlikely observer that, after your lengthy visit to the farm house, Mr. Lassiter is no longer living?" I spoke up.

"It has, Flora," was her answer. "My plan is to leave him there, in that house, until the next day. When I arrive for my usual call, and find that he has passed away, I will send for Doctor Ramsey. Hopefully, no one will try to look in on him after my initial visit; that would be highly unlikely, and it is a chance I am willing to take. As I am the only person he allows in now, I feel relatively safe in that regard."

That decided, we put our heads together to establish the best formula for Vernon Lassiter's release, and agreed on using what was to become a favorite recipe. During our weekly 'whist session' the following day, we mixed pulverized camas with freshly gathered root of cowbane, added a measure of valerian, and sweetened it with our special honey. Mr. Lassiter's departure would be a swift one. Iris was the most adept among us, and we watched with care as she concocted Vernon Lassiter's ticket and presented it to Lily. Her Walter would be proud of his wife: well, at least of her abilities. From within ourselves, we reached out to Lily as she embarked on this solo venture, each of us with her own degrees of relief and anxiety.

Two days later we read in our local newspaper the obituary of Vernon Lassiter, the former farm hand who had lived on, after Ina Schultz had died, at the farm owned by Mrs. Schultz and the late Oscar Schultz. Few people had seen Mr. Lassiter for some time, the article stated, but Doctor Ramsey had kind words for the one person who had cared for the old man. Her ministrations and kindness had surely filled his final days and eased his death, he had said.

Amen.

Two weeks following her loving act for her departed friend, as she sat on the veranda shelling peas for suppertime, Lily received a notice from Daphne's husband. She had been requested to appear at his law office the following afternoon, at three p.m. Peas from her toppled bowl became little green pellets rolling randomly across the porch floor, as she read the legal words which summoned her. Fear made its presence known by the constriction in her stomach and lungs as she wondered how she had possibly been discovered. Who had seen her? Had someone looked through the window and watched as she rocked Vernon Lassiter in her embrace? Could someone have stopped by and seen his body fallen from the rocker, as she had found her friend the day after his death?

Lily had to forcibly calm herself, she told us. Resolution took hold. No matter what happened, fearful as she was, she would remain as disciplined as possible. Lily was the most adept of all of us at being able to compartmentalize and organize her thoughts and feelings. Fortified by her resolve, she deliberately picked up what peas hadn't rolled out of sight, and resumed the calming task of shelling the remaining pods.

Not wishing to bring Daphne into what might, for her, prove to be a compromising situation, Lily had resisted her longing to contact the rest of us. And so, our friend waited the rest of that day and into the next, without revealing to anyone the scenarios spinning inside her head.

———

Lily had met James of course, Janeylib, but did not know him as well as did Iris and I. She was surprised and somewhat offset, she later told us, by his relaxed and friendly greeting as she was shown into his office. Suspicion that she was being primed for unwelcome news, she told us, had set Lily's resolve askew. She obediently sat down on the chair offered her, folded her hands in her lap to control their shaking, futilely tried to clear her mind, and waited for her fate to be determined.

"James regarded some obviously official papers on his

desk," she related at our next whist gathering. "After a few minutes of that, as I sat there dumbly, it felt as if I had been there for half my life. Then, James looked up and smiled again. You surely know Daphne, what a remarkably handsome man you have for a husband," Lily said to Daphne's nodding reply.

"James started by saying that I am a most fortunate woman," Lily went on. "I imagined he meant that I might somehow receive leniency instead of being hanged from the gallows. What he did mean could not have been more of a shock."

"It appears from what I have here," James had begun officially, "that prior to her death, Ina Schultz and Vernon Lassiter were married. Their marriage took place, according to these papers, to assure that the farm and everything on it would be titled to Mr. Lassiter. Furthermore, it is stipulated and agreed to by both parties," James continued, "that, on the death of Vernon Lassiter, everything listed in this document be bequeathed to the daughter of their hearts, namely you, Lily."

"James smiled once more as he reached his hand across his desk to congratulate me, " Lily said as we listened in amazement. "I felt this unexpected news swirling in my addled brain, so many feelings at once, that I simply sat there, stunned. When things began to connect, relief flooded every part of my being, resulting in tears that James mistook for tears of grief. He waited until I was somewhat composed, speaking kind words of condolence mixed with ones of congratulation for my new inheritance. I was in a daze as I signed the offered documents and left James' office. I was not going to stand trial and be imprisoned for the rest of my days. Instead, I was going to be able to access the comforts of that farmhouse whenever I wished, and wrap myself in the remembered warmth of its inhabitants.

Ticket Number Three

Ticket Number Four

It was over a year, Janeylib, before another cry reached our hearts. During that time, Daphne's son was one of many who caught the measles. Daphne was sick with worry as she nursed Frank through weeks of illness and recovery in darkened rooms, fearing that her other children would be infected.

QUARANTINED signs were placed on doors throughout White Laurel as the sickness spread, then finally abated. Iris, who had the measles when we were children, suffered another mild case during the epidemic. But during this time of sickness and loss, a truly happy event occurred. Miracle of miracles, Iris, at the age of thirty-eight, discovered that she was at last to become a mother. I will pass through the time of her confinement, with all its attendant joys and expectations, to the early arrival of Iris and Walter's son. No child had ever been more happily anticipated.

Their baby was born with withered limbs. Within twelve weeks little Luke was determined to be blind and most likely severely brain damaged, as well. Another month of life confirmed this to be the case. He responded only to being held and being fed.

Tussie mussies centered with wilted white roses and tied with purple ribbons arrived at ten on a foggy Tuesday morning. At two in the afternoon, the three of us passed through Iris and Walter's side door.

Walter was working long hours these days, often late into the night, occasionally sleeping through until morning on a cot at the pharmacy. Iris, at home in isolation but for Luke, was dealing with so many feelings at the same time, that they banged into and bounced off each other in her brain. We had seen her totally absorbed in the dear little face of her son at one moment, and railing fiercely in rage during the next. She could become consumed with anger at Walter, anger at herself, anger at God above all others - anger even at the baby himself. Then guilt, the mammoth wave that thunders in with a roar against which all escape is impossible, would drag her out to sea in its powerful undertow and slam her on its rocky shore. She felt irremovable guilt, she said, because she raged against what she had been dealt, demanding from God the things she wished, and for the dark thoughts that filled her nights. The logical, reasoning mind that is a fundamental part of Iris had no place in her life these days. It had been captured beneath raging seas of raw emotion, bits of it rising unrecognized from time to time, to bob on the surface before being caught up and tumbled under again.

We had sat, separately and collectively, many times with Iris and her child during the past few months. But today, we had been summoned.

"I think it was the blindness that began it," Iris said tonelessly when we had gathered, "the fact that Luke would never see my face. I somehow kept imagining that I might cope with everything else, that just maybe I could give my son some semblance of a happy life. Walter had wanted to have him put face down in the pillow, right at the very beginning," she said, looking down at Luke in the cradle his father had made. "I probably will never forgive him for that," she said, "or forgive myself, for silently thinking the same thing way down deep, and letting Walter believe it was only himself having those dark thoughts. Now," Iris intoned, "I see clearly for the first time, that it needs to be done before doing so becomes impossible. Luke needs to return to the Heaven he came from, perhaps to be born again in a different body. God knows, I know, that his life in this one will not be life at all."

She was the Iris we knew that afternoon, with the calm that comes after one's inner wars have found truce, sure of herself and her decision. Then her voice, as she went on speaking, became almost indiscernible. Bending across her table to listen, we heard words ripped from her heart.

"God help me. It is myself I am thinking of in doing this," Iris confessed shakily. At first her voice was barely audible. Gradually, as she went on, it increased in volume. In plangent tones, her words pleaded for nonjudgmental ears to hear them; they could not have reached any more receptive than ours.

"I simply cannot abide my own life being nothing but worse than it is right now," she said, looking from one of us to the next for censure and finding none. "After all those years of convincing myself that it was for the best that I had never conceived, that I didn't really want children in my life, I discovered the opposite to be true. Once my pregnancy was pronounced, I wanted this baby with a desperation that almost scared me. Now, I am just as desperate to send him home. Right now is probably the easiest time of his life, and sometimes it is all, truly all I can do, to keep myself from screaming when I pick him up. Then, just as quickly, I find myself cuddling him and crying tears from a place so deep within me that I never knew it was there, a place I don't want to lose. Until this morning, I have been at the mercy of an internal tornado. My days and nights have become the same to me. I see everything around me in dull shades of gray – I really do. Then this morning, everything cleared. My dark sky parted, revealing a burst of pastel colors, and I knew, with deepest sorrow, what must be done. No matter how I feel at the end of this day, and I can't imagine what that will be, Luke and I will be forever defeated if I don't have the courage to do what certainly is just for both of us, for all of us actually, when I consider Walter. And I don't consider Walter much at all, anymore. I may lose him altogether after this."

"What will you tell Walter?" Lily asked.

"I will tell Walter what I always tell him," Iris replied. "I will tell him the truth."

———

We had agreed, when we began our mission, that whenever possible, one should be given the opportunity to experience one's own death. In this case however, it did not seem fair. Little Luke dozed peacefully, thanks to a light sedative provided by Iris. Held in turn by four pairs of loving arms, then touched by all our hands, the baby son of Iris and Walter drank his final formula in the arms of his loving mother.

———

Because preparations for little Luke's departure had been handled entirely by his mother; because our presence at the station had been limited to our bidding him fare well on his travels to Glory and to sharing the grief of a friend who would not again hold her son in her lifetime; because I loved this woman so deeply that my own unused womb ached with her loss; I have come to terms with this assisticide. In spite of everything, despite my true admiration for my friend's courage and my honor of her choice, I am not sure that I would have made the same decision. In many ways, I hope that I would, but in others, I do not. As is so often the case, either option was the right choice – and the wrong one.

Iris will not read this page. It is one I must include for my own sake, and it will be inserted prior to my delivering this document into James' hands.

Ticket Number Five and, in its own way, Ticket Number Six

From time to time, I love going back to Philadelphia to spend days among friends who stayed in the city after graduating from the Academy. It is a treat to be once again in the company of fellow artists, to catch up with each other's lives, and to taste the flavors of my favorite city. On this one particular trip, I also planned to call upon my dear friend and former professor, Dr. Homer Symthe. I had a particular reason, aside from enjoying his company, for this particular visit. I wanted to recommend admission to the Pennsylvania Academy of the Fine Arts (I love naming this incredible institution) for Millie. I had been thinking for some time about her living room aviary and gallery of owls. Millie's talent was real, and unbeknownst to her, I had come to Philadelphia to plead for her acceptance into the Academy. If anyone could pave the way for her admission, I thought, that person would be my old professor. He had practically founded the place, after all.

Dr. Symthe, a cockalorum of the first order, required some effort to know and ultimately befriend, but behind his manufactured mask of self-esteem, he was a pussycat. A pioneer who first convinced his art department to offer life classes to women, Homer also established exclusive time at the museum for women, two afternoons a week, to draw without interruption from our male counterparts. No wonder that I came to love him.

I remember how skin fascinated him. Attention to details of anatomy was Dr. Symthe's passion, and the manner in which skin stretches, scars, puckers when cold, how it contains pores and follicles from which tiny sensory hairs emerge – all this truly amazed him. He never tired of pointing out on our obliging models ways in which skin conceals, and yet reveals, all that it protects. His bass voice instructed us to capture the body's hidden wonders in our work, to sink our brushes into the blood beneath the dermis, and paint the pulse! Our models were enrobed only in the warmth of his enthusiasm, as their figures liquefied into the paint of our brushes, and transformed themselves to our canvases.

Homer had a second passion, his darling Sally. His wife for many, many years, Sally intimately knew her husband's frustration and disappointment. Somehow, Dr. Symthe could successfully teach, but not apply to his own work, the magic of the brush. His precise renditions of the human form sadly lacked a spark of life. Sally Symthe was herself an accomplished miniaturist, worthy of recognition, but she took great care to let light fall on Homer's accomplishments, rather than on her own. The satisfaction she gained from simply caring for her husband was genuine, and for her, fulfillment enough. As his students, we were welcomed into the Wednesday evening supper events held at the Symthes' home, the highlight of my week. While Homer tended to pontificate, Sally smoothly evened out conversations that often took us well into the night. It was an education in diplomacy to observe them. Mrs. Homer Symthe could have made a wonderful United States President.

In recent years, Homer's work has become recognized. Authors of anatomy and physiology textbooks, as well as a recently published encyclopedia, have commissioned Dr. Symthe's drawings. Finally, in retirement, Homer has gained the stature he deserves.

Sally would have been so happy for him, I thought sadly, as the train pulled into Broad Street Station. As much as I wanted to see them both, I realized that I was bolstering myself for this visit. Now, Homer had recently written to me, Sally no longer recognizes the man who adores her.

When I arrived at their home, Homer called to me from the back of their house, and I went straightaway to Sally's rose garden, a little piece of Paradise nestled into the heart of Philadelphia. It had always been Sally's pride and joy, and would be today, as it was flourishing under her husband's loving care. Sally sat propped up by cushions with a blanket about her, even though the day was not cool, and looked anxiously at her husband. Homer held his wife's hand and asked me to take the seat across from him, so that both of them could see me. It had been a gradual decline, Homer explained, each of them aware, helpless, and terribly frightened as Sally's withdrawal from the world they shared progressed. In some ways, now that she had slipped beyond knowing, her path at least had eased somewhat. She responded only fleetingly to being fed and cared for. He alone bore witness to her state; my visit was the first that he had entertained in many months.

"All those years as sweethearts, Flora, almost sixty years together in marriage, and now it all seems as if it was just a walk around the block. I've had the best a man could possibly know for all that time, and right now, so help me God, I just feel cheated."

We had known each other well, for a very long time, and Harry had known them, too. During that time we had shared many confidences, but I had never told them of the way in which Harry had died, nor of our mission that followed his death. I ached for them both, but my strongest concern was actually for Homer, for he did not look well himself, and I ventured to say so. It was then that he told me, and my day darkened further, of the disease that was consuming his own body. His overwhelming fear was that, when he was gone, there would be no one left to care for Sally; not in the way she deserved, not in the way he was presently able to provide. And his wife was, most likely, going to outlive him. Homer's voice broke as he spoke, and tears spread on his wrinkled cheeks. This man whom I so dearly loved became his age before my eyes.

"I have turned over so many options in my mind, Flora," Homer said that day in the rose garden. "If only Sally and I could leave this world together, I would be content. We have not been apart more than one day since we were married. I can't bear to leave her behind, and I can't take her with me," he said anxiously. "Ending my own life is something I always thought I could do, if I had to - and my end promises to be an agonizing one - but I can't just leave Sally. I have a pistol, and would gladly turn it on myself, but I cannot just shoot the love of my life. I simply cannot."

Homer's head bowed toward his open hands as he finished his lament. He had no idea as to whom he was speaking, or that his words were being carefully registered in my mind and heart. Testing the ground carefully, I expressed no censure regarding his wish to decide his own death; I simply empathized with his difficulty in doing so. My response was not a surprise to him, but it was welcomed nonetheless, as he lifted his gaze to meet mine. I then inquired as to family members or close friends who might be able to care for Sally, and included myself. There was nobody, he replied, his face once more furrowed with anxiety, that could possibly do so. Although Sally was usually calm with him, and with other people while he was present, she became terrified and truly panicked if he was beyond her sight. Putting her in the care of anyone other than himself was unthinkable. She would rather be dead, is what she had told him when they had still been able to talk about what was happening to them both, than to be left in the care of anyone else.

"In that case," I inquired, "if there were a gentler way for Sally to precede you, would you consider sending her on ahead?"

"Absolutely."

Ticket Number Five and, in its own way, Ticket Number Six

Two weeks later, three ladies from White Laurel traveled to Philadelphia for a bit of a holiday. On the second morning of our stay, Lily, Daphne, and I decided to pay a call on one of my former professors. We gathered together with him and his wife in their private rose garden, where Sally became our fifth passenger. Homer cradled her in his lap as he offered our filled spoon, which she licked as if it were a treat. A second spoonful of our own honey, amended for this assisticide with offerings from autumn crocus and lily bulbs, was her reward for finishing the first. Sally's final reward was not long in following.

We left Homer with his wife, as he stroked her face and softly crooned a lullaby, rocking her body gently while he sang. He had requested that he be left alone with her after her departure, and so we quietly clicked the garden gate, and returned to our hotel.

In need of vigorous and exhausting exercise, we prepared to be tourists the following day, but the rest of this one was spent quietly. Lily lit the gas fireplace in our hotel suite and moved closer to it with the book she was reading. Daphne suggested a stroll in the hotel gardens before dinner. Lily preferred some time alone, but promised to join us downstairs presently, and the two of us left for our short tour of the grounds.

⸺

I loved showing 'my' Philadelphia to my friends. Independence Hall and the Liberty Bell, of course, were high on the list that next day, but I especially loved taking them to my very favorite neighborhood, Elfreth's Alley, where all its historic houses were so faithfully maintained. We walked everywhere, purposely exhausting our bodies so that sleep would come more easily than it had the night before. Throughout the day our thoughts and talk returned to Homer Symthe. I had already decided that my trips to this historic city would become more frequent, and I invited my friends to come with me, whenever they liked. Homer would need his friends in the coming weeks. Dinner at Bookbinders was a welcome treat at the end of the day, but we agreed that soaking our weary feet in hot water and salts as we sat on the edge of the bathtub with glasses of sherry, was the ultimate luxury.

At breakfast the next morning, Daphne let out a small cry as she read the morning's newspaper. "Oh Merciful Mary, Mother of God!" she exclaimed. "Flora, Lily, listen to this: 'A tragic murder and suicide have taken place in the rose garden of a former professor who taught at the Pennsylvania Academy of the Fine Arts. A gardener, hired by Dr. Symthe just the day before, discovered the bodies of Dr. Homer Symthe and his wife Sally Harrington Symthe upon his arrival at their property. The professor, when found, still held the pistol that had been fired into his wife's heart before he had turned it on himself, placed it against his right temple, and fired once again.' The article goes on, but how does this make any sense?" Daphne asked. In a voice barely above a whisper, she added, "Sally Symthe had surely boarded the train to Glory before we left. Why on earth would Dr. Symthe have shot her?"

Why, indeed, I wondered, especially as he had told me specifically that this was something he could never do.

As we sat there, amidst the chatter of diners around us, the answer, the only possible answer, came to me. I was so moved that I had to leave the room, and asked the two to join me upstairs when they had finished eating. They followed almost on my heels.

"He did it for us," I explained as they came into our rooms. "He did it to protect us, to shield us from exposure and to protect our mission. It must have been excruciating for Homer to mutilate Sally's beloved body by shooting a bullet into her," and I burst into tears of gratitude and pain.

———

No cause of death, other than that caused by Sally's wounding, was ever remotely considered.

Ticket Number Five and, in its own way, Ticket Number Six

Interlude

Our lives went along uneventfully, Janeylib, for almost a year and a half. Iris did not lose Walter. She had telephoned him at the drug store, she told us, an hour after we had left, following little Luke's departure. It was not her customary habit to ring her husband at work. Walter had not waited to hear the reason for her doing so. When he heard her voice speak his name, he quietly replaced the receiver, hung the sign, locked the door, and went home. Iris said that she hadn't been sure of his response to her call until he entered the house some eternal twenty minutes later, holding daffodils. Tearfully, without revealing any involvement on our part, Iris told her husband what had transpired that afternoon. When she had finished, she said, Walter simply looked at her in solemn silence. Then, rising from where he had been seated, her husband bade her stand, which she did. Walter pulled himself to his highest stature, raised his arms above his head, and brought them down about his wife, encircling her with his strong embrace. He held her closely for the longest time, rocking her back and forth while they sobbed into each other. Then, slowly, he disrobed her, right there in their living room, and Iris found herself doing the same thing for him.

They transported each other that afternoon with tenderness and passion never before experienced or expressed. Depths and heights neither of them had known rose and fell beneath them; their bodies became one with their souls, and their souls spiraled in unison. Later, as they tended the little bundle that had been their son, they did so with solidarity.

As Iris told her tale, my own body throbbed with an unanswered ache. Harry had more than fulfilled his promise of a stellar conjugal partnership, and I strongly missed that part of my life. Daphne smiled her own understanding of Iris' experience, but Lily was clearly uncomfortable during the entire time Iris spoke of her reconciliation with Walter. Surely, Lily knew about these things, even though she had never, so far as we knew, entertained a suitor.

She was still a puzzle sometimes, our Lily. Her life as a teacher of other people's children occupied the better part of her life, and I don't mean just the amount of time involved. She devotes herself to her mother, who still takes over Lily's class on occasion, and to the raising of Anna, her ward. As far as I can tell, her work with us represents the remaining part of her life.

Daphne's elder son was studying to become a lawyer. He had just become engaged, and Daphne had already changed her mind at least a dozen times as to what she should wear to the wedding, even though the event would not take place for another year. She could wear a flour sack, we told her, and still outshine everyone except the bride. Daphne's daughter Patsy wanted to become an actress, or a milliner, or a missionary, depending on her whim of the week. She was twelve now, and starting to look more and more like her mother, lucky girl, even though her coloring was similar to James'. Eliot was Daphne's sensitive, compassionate son, and secretly my favorite child – except of course for you, my dear one. He wangled his way into coming with me one day for a walk in the woods, when I stopped by to see if Daphne would join me. Since she could not, it turned out to be just the two of us who went. Eliot was far more interested in the creatures we encountered than in my drawings, as he sat on the forest's floor and waited for the little animals living there to approach. To my utter amazement, but not to his, a chipmunk actually took bits of bread from the palm of his hand. This is a person with whom I can truly relate, I thought, as the difference in our ages shrank to inconsequence. If he follows his wish to doctor animals when he is grown, his patients will be entrusted into magical hands.

We all loved being privy to the lives of Daphne's children. Their father had fulfilled his desire to become a judge, as my Harry had so strongly hoped would happen. James travels a good deal now, mostly to Philadelphia, allowing Daphne more time with their children, and with us, and with herself.

Lily and Millie have become particular friends. Millie now spends Wednesday afternoons in Lily's classroom, leading Lily's students toward their own explorations into the art world. Millie herself, after conferring with two Academy professors who traveled to White Laurel at the request of the late Dr. Symthe, has decided to continue her work without benefit of their instruction. Flattered, and truly appreciative of their invitation to attend my alma mater, she was nonetheless afraid that her work would begin to look less like her own, and more like creations influenced by her instructors. Suggestions from other artists might befog her own vision, she felt, and that was beyond her realm of acceptance.

"Images born of my brushes," she said to them, "need to be mothered by me alone. I don't wish my work to be something that is taught, or to have my concepts overlaid by those of other painters. I do not expect you to understand," she emphasized, " that which to me is beyond understanding. The illustrated rooms you have witnessed portray the years of my life that were spent in relative solitude, years during which their walls' embellishment ensured my sanity. My precious birds need to fly free, in skies unclouded by others' intrusions."

Whether or not they comprehended her reasons, the two professors reluctantly returned to Philadelphia without a new student. They did take with them small works of Millie's choosing, reward enough for their journey, they claimed, and told her that their offer would remain open. Perhaps Millie's mind has grasped a kite string of wisdom that the rest of us have somehow missed, or overlooked.

The four of us really do play whist on Thursdays, after Lily has finished teaching for the day, and we have also branched into the study of mushrooms. The further we researched the ones found in our woods, the more convinced we became that mushrooms had no place in our compendium. They are much too detectable for our purposes, we decided, and most of them offered far too nasty a demise. But it is a darkly fascinating study.

Permissions to visit our Norris 'Grandmother's Flower Garden' quilt have become increasingly sought by horticulturists and everyday gardeners who wish to view them, so we decided to permit scheduled visitors on six afternoons a month. Eight Floraphiles, who have regularly maintained the gardens, happily got up from their knees and became docents. They are justly proud of their work, and delight in showing it off. Those who seek to venture beyond the gates of the Doctor's garden are denied access. Our restricted bees need protection from intrusion, is the explanation these folk are given.

—

Life was lovely during this time, a bit dull perhaps, but that in itself was truly pleasant. Excitement is not my preferred state of being, and time periods surrounding an assisticide are fraught with all kinds of justifiable fears and sleepless nights.

Illustrations for a new volume on the wildflowers of the Pocono Mountains received full attention, filled much of my days, and led me beyond my persistent longings for Harry. I did so want to move beyond the life I still pined for, to fully embrace the life I now had.

Interlude

Ticket Number Seven
and Ticket Number Eight

The Misses Pearl and Ruby Schumacher. Identical twins, these women had been born to our local butcher, who was known as a truly gentle man, and to his querulous wife, whose temperament did not match that of her husband. The twins' father doted on the girls, and pretty much raised them, while his wife kept the accounts, ran the shop, and supervised her husband. This arrangement seemed to have worked well for the adult Schumachers, who devoted themselves to each other, and ran both a thriving business and successful household. Their twins looked so much alike that they routinely baffled grownups, including their own parents - much to the girls' delight. Mrs. Schumacher dressed the two in identical outfits. She parted their hair in the middle, above their widow's peaks, and fashioned thick auburn braids that were then looped and tied with ribbon; sometimes, the ribbon was braided in with their hair, and then fashioned into bows at their ears. They walked, spoke, and smiled as if one girl was real and the other a mirror image. Canoeing on the Lehigh River in their bloomers and middies, the sisters, I had been told, plied the parting waters as a unit, as two people forming a single paddling force. Ruby and Pearl have navigated lakes and rivers throughout the world since their girlhood, but still claim the Lehigh as their favorite river of all. Photographs of the two, usually clad in versions of the outfits worn by them as girls, have appeared in publications from places far beyond the borders of White Laurel. In our town, the Schumacher sisters have achieved reputations that vary according to the eyes and minds of their perceivers. They have experienced both applause and censure. After all, they do wear trousers and smoke Imperials through tortoise shell cigarette holders! Pearl and Ruby were women whom my own mother adored, thereby coming under the veil of criticism herself. 'Too bad, for those who miss out on knowing them,' I recall her telling me. Now in their later years, they continued to live in the family house on Berwyn Street, and still canoed from their dock into the familiar waters of the Lehigh.

It was Miss Pearl who summoned me by messenger one early November morning. No invitation, no written request, just their two-horse carriage and its driver that waited while I covered Caruso's cage, snatched my duster from its hook, pinned on a hat, and sailed out my front door. My curiosity was only moderately contained while the distance between my house and theirs seemed quickly achieved, and I soon found myself handed down from the carriage by its driver.

I stood alongside the carriage puzzled, as my eyes adjusted to seeing the Schumacher house. I had known it for years, but had apparently paid little or no attention to it before now. Stark, is the word that registered in my mind. Whitish gray, set high and far back from the road, flanked by cement walkways and pale gray gravel, the narrow structure of the house appeared foreboding. Rising that morning against a backdrop of overcast sky, the house seemed on the verge of disappearing altogether. Unrelieved by fencing or foliage of any kind, the poor place stood naked against the elements, bones exposed to the whims of nature. Odd, I thought, that its colorful inhabitants would choose to surround themselves with such lackluster nothingness.

The front door, when it opened as I still stood near the carriage, presented the tall, thin form of Miss Pearl. Against a surround of deep green walls, enhanced by the glow of gaslight from her sconces, she stood centered against a block of color, a pearl set in emerald. Planned or not, the effect was astonishing.

Lightly descending her porch steps, Miss Pearl hurried

down the walkway to take my arm and, patting it all the way while thanking me for coming on no notice at all, she led me through that doorway into a vestibule walled in a forest of felt. I tend to be a bit claustrophobic, and was relieved to pass quickly into the front parlor, where birch logs fed flames in a small tiled fireplace. The carved mantelpiece above the fireplace shelved silver framed photographs of various sizes, while cherubs climbed and peeked from vines cast into tiles that formed the surround. Small vases of flowers, mostly roses, were tucked all about the room. That was a surprise. It was a bit late for roses. Where had they come from? The parlor walls above the wainscoting were also covered in fabric. Here, a rich moire, pale dove gray in color, softly absorbed and reflected shades of upholstery and costumes worn within the room. Fire-light wanded its magic over all, giving bursts of brilliance to an otherwise subdued surrounding. Above tall narrow windows, smaller ones of stained glass had been positioned like coronets, a feature that the firelight loved. Miss Pearl watched with interest as my gaze took in one unexpected feature after another. I felt as though I had passed through a protective rind to the interior of a luscious fruit. Miss Pearl laughed lightly when I told her this. My reaction was not an uncommon one, she said, although she had not before heard it so poetically expressed.

I was directed to sit on one of the four horsehair chairs, softened, thankfully, with emerald green velvet upholstery, and antimacassared with ivory crochet. It was set before a low marble topped table, close to the comforts of the fire. Miss Pearl took the second chair, while the third and fourth, for the moment, remained unoccupied. She bent at the waist, and our eyes met.

By now, our circle had found these kinds of summons to generally become appeals for our help. On most occasions, our decision was to support the seeker through a natural course of events without benefit of assistance. This, I felt, was not to be one of those times. As if in answer to my forming wish that another of our circle would be present, the doorbell rang. Iris, a bit out of breath, had been summoned just as I had. Obviously relieved to see me there, my friend was invited to take the third chair, and after sweeping her curious and appreciative eye about the parlor, Iris' solemn countenance came to rest on that of our hostess. Miss Pearl, apparently not expecting a third visitor, sensed our desire to learn the reason for our gathering and turned her attention toward us.

"I have a story to tell, and then a request to make," Miss Pearl began ceremoniously, "and have written down what I have to say, so that I will not omit, and so that you may share, as necessary. You may interrupt if you feel the need, but I pray that you will hear me through to the end."

Iris and I shared not unnoticed glances.

"Ruby and I are identical, and yet opposite in ways other than our appearance," Miss Pearl began. "At times, we have hated this, and illogically each other for it; yet it is a truth that holds us in awe. If one of us develops a cavity, the other surely has one in the same tooth, but on the other side" Miss Pearl looked from Iris to me, and then went on. "We began womanhood on the same day, within the same hour, terrified that we were dying until Father consoled us and gently explained what was happening. He must have practiced his speech again and again," Miss Pearl mused, "in order to have done it so well. If one of us was in trouble, the other twin sensed it. If one of us became ill, the other succumbed as well. This happened even during the rare occasions that we were apart."

The tea tray, for which Miss Pearl had rung, arrived and was placed on the table before us. Miss Pearl nodded, and peppermint scented tea was poured into primrose patterned china cups. I have always been partial to peppermint. Do you remember our tea parties with the fairies, Janeylib? Down in the center of the gardens by the red maple?

"Three times," Miss Pearl went on, "our parents divided us by sending Ruby to visit one set of relatives while I went to another. This was not done unkindly, but for our benefit, they believed. During the first trial, when Ruby sprained her left ankle in uncle's pasture, I suddenly felt such severe pain in my right leg that I tripped and sprained that ankle. Later, Ruby and I compared the exact time, and day, that we were injured. Neither of us was surprised at the coincidence, but our parents were visibly disturbed by it.

On the second attempt at separation, we were sent to opposite sets of grandparents, and proceeded to develop chickenpox our second week into the visit. All four grandparents laughingly swore later that their children had undoubtedly planned it that way. Ruby and I recovered on the same day and we each bear identical, but opposite, scars on our foreheads." Miss Pearl placed a long finger to her temple, directed toward a faint circular mark. "Both Ruby and I longed for each other during that whole itchy experience, but agreed that we'd had more fun with Nana and Gran than we would have had at home. We were even allowed to keep our 'QUARANTINED' signs; we still have them up in the attic along with our other treasures."

Miss Pearl's expression had softened during her recollection of that visit, whilst Iris and I listened with anticipation for her next revelation. Never once had she referred to the papers at her side, nor did she now. She stood for a moment to retrieve a flat cushion from her davenport, which she placed beneath her before sitting once more, and remarked apologetically about her 'old bones', while sliding down a bit to reduce her added height. Iris raised her brows in my direction. I answered with a brief shrug. Miss Pearl politely ignored our gestures, and resumed speaking.

"We were older," she said solemnly, "when the third attempt was made. We had exchanged grandparents from our last visit, my being with Nana and Dad this time, and Ruby with Gran and Grampa Ed. Something peculiar began to happen within me that summer. It wasn't a physical change, although it certainly seemed so at times, but a change I now recognize as personal growth. Windows and doors within me opened while others closed, slipped away, and vanished. Parts of me melted away, to be replaced by unfamiliar parts whose time to be had arrived. Apart from my twin, in relative solitude, I experienced an internal transition. Like water on a desert, my unknown thirst for selfhood was being slaked.

For several minutes the three of us sat, lost in thought, with only the occasional snap of firewood unsettling the silence. I contemplated the alterations each of the four of us had experienced during the past few years. Some of my own changes had slipped in quietly, their existence realized at odd moments, often, but not always, with surprise. Once in a great while, a quiet flow takes place within me, and I ride its currents. Reluctance to leave shore leaves me stagnant, so I have learned to step onto the shifting sands of change, and trust the gods. Such is the case with everyone, I had thought. Today, I am less sure.

What was my Iris thinking? I wished that I knew.

"That was our seventeenth summer," Miss Pearl continued, just before we turned eighteen." She paused, gathering herself before going on. "I fell forever in love that summer, with a piano student of Nana. Ernest was four years my senior, a serious student of music, and about to enter his final year at university. He was handsome, actually taller than I, and my match in both intelligence and yen for adventure. Nana and Dad were both delighted with our good fortune. By the end of my visit with them, Ernest and I had become engaged to marry. Certain that Ruby had experienced similar changes that summer, I wrote to her of mine and of my coming marriage to Ernest. Nothing could have prepared me for Ruby's response. Her summer, she wrote in return, had been spent spiraling slowly downward into a melancholy from which nothing had been able to divert her. My letter, although it should have cheered her, created a crushing sense of loss. Our mother had been sent for, and her admonishment for Ruby to 'Snap out of it!' resulted in further low spirits. She had truly tried, Ruby wrote, and was honestly pleased for me. Her melancholy, however, refused lifting." Miss Pearl sat very still, reliving a pain only partially lost. In a voice edged with that memory, she willed herself to go on.

"My twin rallied somewhat," she said, "after we returned home. She busied herself with my wedding preparations and, when our wedding day came, walked before me down the aisle of the church as I approached the man I loved. As I began my vows to Ernest, after he had spoken his to me, Ruby fell to my feet in a dead faint. She had actually stopped breathing. I put my mouth to hers and breathed for both of us while my almost-husband waited. My choice of life partner changed in those few seconds before Ruby responded to my breath. We two have been together ever since, as surely we were born to be," Miss Pearl concluded in a firm voice.

Iris and I, along with Lily and Daphne, had heard many stories since the start of our ministry. This one left Iris and me speechless in our chairs. It was Iris who, in her matter of fact way, broke the silence by asking for both of us, "What became of Ernest?"

"He died of consumption two years, three weeks, and four days later."

Miss Pearl rearranged her angular body, and shifted it so that she could look out through her south-facing window. She was thereby afforded the unobstructed view of her sloping lawn and the river that lay beyond it. The Lehigh was swollen, I had noticed from the carriage, thinking it a wise plan that the Schumacher house had been built safely above it. The launching of canoes was easily managed from the dock at the base of the property, especially when waters were as they now appeared. It has always been a favorite, although forbidden, spot for local children to jump into the welcoming waters, and play at hide-and-seek around the canoes. Miss Ruby and Miss Pearl paid lip service to the perils of children playing there, but it was really quite safe, as the water there is usually not deep, and all river children are swimmers. I think that a bit more concern was lent to what might have taken place beneath those canoes.

Time, interrupting my reverie, shuffled from the folds of plum velvet drapery with a yawn. An hour in Miss Pearl's presence had seemed to take up the whole afternoon, when in reality, it was still quite early. Iris' recent loss of weight was accompanied by increased energy, and sitting still had never been easy for her, even when she was heavy. She shifted repeatedly in her chair despite her conscious efforts to remain politely relaxed. I had less difficulty than she at maintaining my composure, but did wish that Miss Pearl would soon come to the reason for our having been summoned.

———

Miss Ruby's arrival abruptly altered the entire atmosphere. She swung open the door from their kitchen with a bump of her rump, carrying, as if an offering to the gods, a large silver tray piled with an array of finger sandwiches and little lemon frosted cakes. Unceremoniously depositing the tray on the table before us, Miss Ruby greeted Iris, then me, with the French kiss-without-touching of cheeks, making little smacking sounds into the air. As Miss Pearl had done, she took our hands in hers and warmly thanked us for coming. Now, crustless little sandwiches are a favorite of mine, but they waited on their tray while I feasted my eyes on the still remarkable resemblance of the Schumacher sisters. Mannerism, appearance, voice and costume were twin in each respect, and yet I detected shades of difference, shifts of humor and authority. This afternoon, they were dressed in full cut raspberry silk trousers that actually looked like skirts, and middy tops in a deep mustard tone of the same fabric, trimmed in raspberry. I should have liked planting the two of them in my garden just to see them grow and watch their petals unfurl.

Gazing beyond Miss Ruby while she poured fresh tea, I noticed for the first time a painting hung near the doorway to the vestibule. I beckoned Iris to join me, and together we excused ourselves to cross the room for a closer look. Portrayed were the twins, wearing the same costumes in which they were dressed this afternoon. They stood together on their dock, grasping a single canoe paddle held vertically, hands placed one above the other as if they were playing a game to see whose fingers would first reach the top. Ruby and Pearl looked directly at us from the canvas, glints of defiance piercing their painted eyes, bemused expressions inviting our interpretations. Amazing. The artist sought participation from the viewer, as an author does her reader. Alongside Miss Pearl a blue jay perched on a leafless branch, head tilted as his birdy eye took in the look-alike women standing there. Those three had a secret.

"Whose work is this?" I asked, for I saw no signature, although I surely suspected the answer.

The Misses Ruby and Pearl, watching from their chairs affirmed my conjecture. "Mildred Harper's."

There was no longer any ambivalence as to why we were here. Millie had sent us. Surely, the roses dotting the room had been delivered by her, hothouse roses, her very own. Had Millie betrayed us? Well known fears began their intrusion, as the sisters' carefully planned plea for assisticide began to unfold.

"We began bleeding." Miss Ruby's voice interrupted my thoughts. "I started first, and within the hour, Pearl's began, just as had happened so many years before. Except that this time, there was no consolation, no reassurance of this being a natural process. Years ago, we feared our bleeding meant the beginning of our ends. This time, we suspected that fear to be valid. Visits to Doctor Ramsey did not prove us wrong. After all the indignities of the examinations, he announced that our female parts, which we did not get to use during our lifetimes, would be the death of us. Operations might buy us a little more time, he told us, but would sap our remaining strength. We had already lost some weight and would assuredly lose more, before the truly difficult trial of dealing with our disease begins. He would honor our decisions for treatment, but we are beyond curing."

———

A heightened perception of all surrounding me, the quickening flame of anticipation I experience when beginning an ending, sprang to life. Feelings both fascinating and frightening were moving from the fringes of my mind; the request had not been made, but the reaction had begun. Iris was looking directly toward me, her inner gaze focused elsewhere. Little Luke rose within her each time our help was sought, she had told me, lending her his strength and resolve. Practical and patient, Iris assumed total calm at these moments, and began to focus on formulating a plan of departure for our prospective passengers.

———

"We wish," Miss Ruby continued, having received a dismissive wave of hand from her sister, "to have you and a few guests join us for a Sunday afternoon picnic by the river. It's an unusual time of year for a picnic, but still, the weather is enjoyable. I believe that two of your Floraphile friends might care to join us, and I have already spoken with Mildred."

———

The stab of alarm registered by Iris was echoed in my own breast. Just what and how much had Millie revealed? We would surely go to the gallows for the work we did. Only our passionate conviction that assisticide was a merciful act allowed us to brave the consequences that society imposed. We risked our own lives with each passenger's leave-taking. Surely Millie realized that. She could have been implicated herself, in the departure of her own mother, for Lord's sake. Could she have jeopardized all of us in order to befriend the women with whom we sat this afternoon? With a great deal of difficulty, Iris and I maintained impassive expressions, and waited as Miss Pearl consulted the papers in her lap. Mildred Harper, it appeared, when she again spoke, had only suggested that Iris and I be taken into their confidence before the sisters carried out their own plan. My moments of anxiety, although still a force, had abated somewhat, but Millie's suggestion still carried overtones of treachery.

———

"Would we care to join them at a riverside repast before she and Ruby launched their canoe for a final paddle?"

"Ah," breathed Iris, immediately snatching unspoken thoughts out of the crowded air. Raising her brows to me for confirmation, answered by my relieved nod, Iris proceeded to gently question, as only Iris can. " And by 'final', Miss Pearl, "do you mean that you have decided to retire your paddles?"

The twins regarded Iris more keenly. "They will be used no more."

Subtly shifted to the panes below them, rampant rays of orange and gold passed unhampered through the bubbled glass of the stained glass coronets.

"And the canoes themselves?" Iris asked.

"There will be just one, which we will paddle together," Miss Pearl replied calmly. "The other has its future home already decided. Ruby and I have, for years, wondered what it would be like to plunge across the Lehigh's dam," she added casually.

Clouds softened the sun's rays and muted their light. Despite heat from the hearth, I felt a sudden, familiar chill.

"The thrill of the idea has captured us more than once," Miss Ruby picked up, "whenever we have come anywhere near the dam. Twice, we came too close for comfort, and paddled furiously in order to avoid going across. Each time, we were increasingly intrigued by the thought of joining the falling waters rushing finitely toward the rocks waiting to receive us. What better way to meet our Maker than by fulfilling an earthly desire as we enter His Kingdom?"

It appeared to me that the Schumacher twins had already decided their dramatic demise, and my mood shifted. Any attendance by us at their farewell picnic would simply be socially supportive.

Iris suspected otherwise, however, and spoke her final question almost as if it were a statement.

"There is some difficulty with your plan?"

Miss Ruby studied Iris with visible admiration. "The possibility exists, Iris, however remote it might be, that one or both of us could survive this experience. That cannot be allowed. Or left to chance."

Her sister nodded, eyes closed, her fingers curled about the papers still in her lap, as Miss Ruby went on.

"We wish assurance that as we cross the dam, we are approaching oblivion. When we came to this place in our story while speaking with Mildred, she suggested our revealing it to you. Why she did so is a mystery to us both, but here we all are at the end of this beautiful day, putting the question to you and to Flora. What time Pearl and I have left, we wish to live well. Right to the very end."

A crossing glance between the two of us resulted in Iris and myself getting up from our chairs, and leaving the coziness of the cherub-tiled fireplace and the close company of the Schumacher sisters. Cooler air immediately cleared my mind and ended our afternoon. We would, I told the still unanswered twins, respond to their dilemma in three days time. Would they be at home to receive? They would.

The Misses Ruby and Pearl Schumacher waved from their doorway as we stepped into their waiting carriage, and we looked back on the house blending against the evening sky as its door was closed, protecting its precious jewels and their secrets within its luscious interior.

———

Lemon geranium and ivy leaves nested bits of borage, sage, and bee balm in the following morning's tussie mussies. An unexpected meeting of trusting friends, required to speak their own minds, maintain compassion, and exercise wisdom was scheduled for that afternoon. Knots in the purple ribbon set the time at two o'clock.

Thursday, being our regular whist day, Janeylib, made a trip to the Schumachers easily arranged, but meetings hastily called for planning were sometimes unattended by one or more of us. Four concurring votes were required to determine a performance of assisticide, while two of us could work together to prepare the tickets to Glory. None of us was to act completely alone. For this meeting, Daphne had sent a small bouquet of everlasting pea, striped carnation, and astilbe. She was unable to attend, and would await our pleasure.

———

Lily, as usual, had arrived before the appointed time and was busy helping Iris when I arrived. We settled in my favorite spot in Walter and Iris' house, a little breakfast nook just off their kitchen, where the yellow and white checkered tablecloth was set for four, in case Daphne showed up after all, I assumed. The windowsill was scattered with shells and small stones, relics of Iris and Walter's wanderings along beaches and pathways. We were long past noticing each other's housekeeping, but Iris, as usual, apologized for not having moved the dust around and polished the windows. Lily and I both rather envied Iris' relaxed attitude toward household chores, and once again tossed aside her remark. I don't recall Iris ever having employed servants, and apparently, she and Walter were quite comfortable performing their own household duties by themselves. We were lucky this morning, for Iris had baked her raisin-molasses muffins and they perfumed the air of her kitchen. Flanked by squat jars of late marigolds and set alongside butter, marmalade, and a pot of coffee, the muffins enticed us to devour them. Sunshine, flowers, and treats from Iris' kitchen were a warm and welcome contrast to the reason for this morning's meeting.

Although Daphne had indicated her concurrence with whatever we agreed upon, today's decision was made more precarious because of Millie's involvement, and I found myself wishing that Daphne had been able to join us. I had many questions and misgivings as far as Millie was concerned, even though I personally hoped to be able to aid Miss Ruby and Miss Pearl.

We did not easily or casually select our passengers, Janey-lib, although our agreement to aid them could sometimes be quickly reached. We acted only after thorough discussion, and unanimous concurrence. Pricks of anxiety, in the consideration to be decided today, deeply etched the word 'caution' on my brain.

As regularly happened, Iris picked up on my thoughts. "Millie is going to be with us this morning, Flora. You are not the only one who has questions for her. I told Lily, before you arrived, about the canoeing twins and their plan for a dam dive, and about Millie's suggestion that we be there for the send-off. What more Millie may have told them in regards to us is something I mean to find out. She should be here in another half hour, so let's have some coffee and figure out just what to ask her before she arrives."

With that we decided, after Lily's calm suggestion that we do so, was that we should first listen to what Millie had to say for herself. After that, our discussion centered on the Schumacher twins themselves, and on their enviable attitudes toward living. Iris' coffee is always strong, and a perfect background for cream. The muffins were wrapped in a kitchen towel and left to stay warm in the oven, but we each did sample just one. In the interim we discussed recipes that would work for the launching of the Schumacher sisters. They wanted to be fully

aware of their experience, which ruled out valerian and lau-
danum. Castor would work well, as would camas, foxglove,
yew or monkshood. Distilled essences of one or two of these
mixed into honeyed brandy would provide a proper farewell
toast before the Schumacher sisters took their plunge into ob-
scurity. Yes, amended brandy would be the perfect ticket for
these adventurous women! If we agreed to proceed, we would
decide the exact formula the following morning and begin its
preparation. On Thursday afternoon, some of us would pay a
call on the two jewels who lived in the disappearing house on
the hill.

———

As so often happens, the stew of anxiety and anger brewed
up within Iris and myself was tempered by the cooling breath
of explanation. Millie, prior to her arrival, had suspected the
reason for her having been invited this morning. Seated now
among us, and buoyed by Iris' muffins and coffee, she told us
about her having been summoned by 'the girls'.

"They have been mothers to me, even before my own
mother took ill," Millie began, brushing crumbs from her chin,
"and after my mother took to her bed, they were my link to
the world beyond my prison. Without them and their encour-
agement, I'm not sure how, or if, I would have survived those
interminable years of caring for Isobel. It now feels a lifetime
since she died, which it is actually, since the existence I knew
then has vanished forever."

Millie looked up from the hands in her lap and encountered faces inviting her to go on.

"I have known for some time that they are ill," she continued. "I didn't know how ill until they told me their thoughts
about a final canoe ride. Now, I have witnessed some of what
others deem the eccentricities of 'those daft Schumacher
twins', and I've seen them stung by remarks best not heard.
I have envied their freedom, their appetite for whatever life
dishes up and puts on their platter. I cherish the evenings I

spent listening to stories of rapids on foreign rivers and the teamwork needed to maneuver them, of sweating bodies and bug bites, of frosty banks and frigid fingers that paddled from memory. Theirs was a world I could only imagine. It was a storybook, and they took me into it. After their visits, I would go up to the third floor and record their perils and delights on my walls, and there, I could join them. I painted myself into their canoes, pressed my image into a riverbank, and sat beside a spotted owl in the moonlight, perched on a limb high above my adventurers. I went to the Adirondacks, paddled the Snake, saw moonlight on the Canyon walls, felt the heaviness of African heat, and the sweet familiarity of the Lehigh."

Millie's voice rose and fell as she held us spellbound. At times it had quavered. Now, she startled us as she cried out "I didn't live *through* these amazing women – I lived *because* of them!" she said with a constricted voice. Dammed tears broke free and made rivulets that Millie spoke through. "I would do anything for them, absolutely anything, including helping them to die," she declared. "If you decide to help them, I implore you, allow me to be a part of it," and she finished, her voice wrenched, "Please."

This was an entirely unexpected twist in a mission that has been full of all sorts of unforeseen events. Waiting for Millie's tears to subside, watching as she was wrapped first in Lily's arms, then in a warmed shawl as she calmed herself, we turned her request about in our minds. My personal empathy for Millie did not cancel my need to know just what it was that she had told Miss Pearl and Miss Ruby regarding Daphne, Iris, Lily, and Camas. And so, as calmly as I could do so, I prepared to ask her. This time, however, it was Lily's words that eclipsed my own.

"What, exactly, Millie, did you have to say to your friends about our mission?" she asked pointedly, then immediately followed with, "When they told you of their intentions, why on earth did you bring up the Floraphiles? Don't you realize the appalling risks the four of us take? We live with very real fear in our hearts each and every day. We certainly don't need more!"

Lily's words snapped through the air like whip-cracks. So much for her remaining calm!

"I myself feel downright betrayed," she continued, "and I imagine that is how my friends feel, as well." With that, Lily sat back, eyes flashing like railroad blinkers waiting for the proper signals.

A touch of her own anger was exactly what Millie needed to re-enforce her resolve. Directly and defiantly, she replied without skipping a breath. "Because I love them, Lily. Surely, that is something that you can understand," she shot back with a knowing glance. "Furthermore, I did not betray any one of you. I would have been less than loyal to Ruby and Pearl, and I believe to all of you, had I not suggested your hearing their story. You are anxious about the security, as well as the sanctity, of your mission. Well, so am I. My going to Ruby and Pearl was no more incriminating than Harry's coming to me. Have you forgotten Harry's recommendation that I seek Flora's aid when my mother's condition became desperate? Harry never told me that Flora would help me, only that she would hear me, and she did. You were a godsend, each and all of you. You still are. And, I deeply wish to involve myself in this final act of mercy for Ruby and Pearl, danger be damned. Taking part would be an honor, for me, as well as a holy act of love."

With that said, Millie sat back, took a huge bite from a muffin, and chewed solidly while the three of us digested her speech. She swigged it down with a gulp of leftover coffee, and took another bite. Still eyeing us defensively as she picked up crumbs from the table by pressing a finger against them, Millie maintained her silence.

Iris was the first of us to stir, and she spoke with startling brightness. "How about some nice, fresh coffee," she suggested. She refilled the pot and passed it, but nothing more was said as we poured, sugared, creamed, and stirred.

"Perhaps it is best that I leave," Millie ventured, her out-pouring only partially abated. Her voice was less strident, her shoulders squared, as she pushed herself away from the table.

"No, no, Millie," I told her, placing my hand lightly on her arm, feeling her resistance. "Please, sit."

Lily and Iris sat impassively across from us as I turned to face Millie. Hearing about Harry's advice to her all those years back had unnerved me, but Millie had made a valid point. I asked whether she would allow the three of us a little time to confer without her presence. Would she agree to our excusing ourselves while she waited? Millie nodded gracefully, and we adjourned to the coolness of Iris' living room. A telephone call to Daphne gave us assurance that she could join us in the morning to wind bandages for wounded soldiers, our code for meeting in the laboratory. The number of clicks along the line as we disconnected underscored our need to be cautious, and we always kept a ready supply of rolled bandages ready for donation, to offset suspicions. Millie had brought into direct focus the fears of our work being discovered. We zealously regarded our practice as noble and needed work. Assisticide is more than an act of mercy; it is a supreme act of love. But discovery would be fatal, literally, for all of us, and just as importantly, for our mission. Would the addition of Millie for this one passage to Glory be an offsetting advantage, or an unwise inclusion?

Lily still had strong concerns over the wisdom of allowing Millie to participate. I couldn't erase Harry from the equation, which overshadowed my ability to think clearly. Iris truly thought that Millie's involvement would alter our pattern and provide diversion, thus distracting from possible suspicions. Ultimately, since we agreed that Millie had in fact committed no true indiscretion, and that her deep desire to aid those she loved was genuine, we guardedly opted to honor her request.

First to return to the kitchen, Lily sat beside her friend, and extending both hands, delivered the news that Millie had hoped to hear.

"You cannot begin to fathom, Millie, the depth of the decision you are making," Lily said solemnly. "When all of this began for us, I thought it would be as if I were turning from a familiar path onto a new road. In reality, I was stepping from the edge of a cliff into an unknowable void. Every assisticide becomes another free-fall as the branch you have somehow managed to grab gives way, and you plummet farther into this act that, although merciful, is a bottomless undertaking. I realize that you were a part of Isobel's departure, but she was your mother, and you, an intimate part of her life. Dealing with passengers outside our own familial frameworks presents an entirely different dimension. No matter that we firmly believe in the sanctity of assisticide. There still exists the fact that we aid people in their deaths; we alter our ticket holders' appointed times of departure. Is God working through our hands, or are we playing God's hand? We don't know. We will never know."

Iris and I echoed Lily's words to her friend. Each of us had known the dichotomy in our minds and hearts concerning the work we performed. We had individually come to terms with our turmoil, but nothing made it go away.

"If you can join us in the morning at Flora's house, Millie," Iris said after shifting her again-rounding self on her seat, "at a quarter past nine, we shall decide the formula for the Schumacher twins' final draught. The three of us will confer with Daphne prior to your arrival. In this instance, we have decided that if even one among us is not in favor of your participation, her nay vote is decisive. Can you accept this and be with us in the morning?"

Millie's defensive mien vanished. Seated with us now was the woman we all admired and had grown to care for.

"I will be there, and thank you, each of you. I hope you know that I would never, ever, betray or compromise your outreach. I truly believe that I have not done so. Now, if you will excuse me, I must return to my work."

"One thing, before you go," Lily asked for all of us, "Will

you allow us to visit your third floor?"

Millie paused before answering, and lightly bit her lower lip while entertaining our request.

"The walls of the room where Pearl and Ruby will forever reside are not yet completed," she said slowly. "A sizable section of one wall remains untouched. It is my wish that each of you will occupy a portion of that space. I am reluctant to show unfinished projects, so, at this juncture, I must say 'no' to your wishes. At some point in the future, I am hopeful that my answer will be a different one. I look forward to seeing you in the morning. Thank you, Iris, for your hospitality. If you care to share receipts, I would love to have the one for your muffins. They are wonderful."

With that, Janeylib, Millie was gone, and the day had been toppled on its head. Surely, no more was to be accomplished before morning, so we gathered our tools and spent the rest of the afternoon in blessed physical labor among the defunct chrysanthemums in the fading autumn quilt of Norris Gardens.

———

Daphne, when she arrived at my home the next morning, bustled in all out of breath, out of sorts and out of temper. James had been offered an opportunity to combine his White Laurel law practice with that of a prestigious firm in Philadelphia, which would require James' living in Philadelphia more days than at home in White Laurel. And he had accepted their offer! Without his even discussing it with her! And he expected his wife to be overjoyed! Daphne was incensed. Her Irish temper had flared. His German inflexibility had raised its stupid head and tried to 'reason' with her, which infuriated her further. The words she let slip from her tongue before he left had not been filtered through her brain.

"I said dreadful things to him, and meant every single one of them," she told us hotly. "James barely listened, if he heard me at all. 'Daphne, Daphne,' he kept saying, as if I didn't know my own name. I stood blocking his way when he left this morning for the city, and he simply lifted me up from the sidewalk and set me to the side. This is my life that James is toying with, not just his own, and he doesn't recognize that I even have one! Aside from this mission we are devoted to, I hardly recognize a life of my own, myself," she said, and her face registered shock at hearing the sound of her own words express thoughts she had not consciously entertained.

We had long ago become listeners, not advisors to one another, and this time was no different. Daphne just needed to hear herself and form her own decisions. Her pretty copper curls framed a face flushed with Irish indignation, as she plopped herself down and reached for the coffeepot.

"I am so glad to be here," she said, shifting her focus. "It feels wickedly good to be plotting while James is off dealing with laws and justice. If only he knew how his wife spends time with her friends," she said offhandedly to three suddenly stricken faces, "but that, it goes without saying, he never will. Alrighty, now. What are we going to do for the Schumacher ladies?"

Iris related the stories told by Ruby and Pearl, and then of their conundrum concerning possible survival after their trip across the dam. As for our concerns over Millie's request to be part of this particular send-off, Daphne, fully involved now with the issue at hand, asked for an explanation to our misgivings. After Lily expressed our thoughts, Daphne agreed, by all the saints, with our concern for caution. We'd had the luck of the Irish up to this point.

Privately, Janeylib, I thought it was more than luck, as Doc Ramsey was a bright and observant physician, and his remarks after the passage of Vernon Lassiter had stayed in my mind. He had spoken of Lassiter's death being 'eased', and I felt that we were being monitored. As close as John Ramsey had been to Harry and me, he was a dedicated and scrupulous doctor. Even though we exercised every possible means of vigilance, the possibility of discovery accompanied every act of assisticide, and lingered long beyond the deed.

"As far as including Millie during our preparations," Daphne's voice broke into my thoughts, "I actually think it a wise consideration. First of all, she didn't actually reveal our mission, so let's put that to rest. Secondly, her presence will off-set our customary pattern, which in turn may offset unforeseen suspicions. Thirdly, including Millie will usurp any unlikely re-sentment and possible retaliation that she might have should we deny her request. I don't like harboring that particular fac-tor, but there it is. Fourth, in number only, I personally trust her, and I admire tremendously her ability to go forward with her own life in spite of all that she has had to deal with."

"James is not the only one in your family to have a ratio-nal mind, Daphne," remarked Iris. "He will be hard pressed to deal with whatever you have in store for him, when he comes home from Philadelphia!"

Daphne managed a laugh, ran her hand smoothly across her sprigged linen skirt, and rose to answer my doorbell. Millie proved prompt as usual, having stood, I suspected, until the precise moment before turning the bell key. In she stepped, to four welcoming women waiting to respond to her request to help the Schumacher twins depart from the waters of this world.

Millie went alone, the following day, to call on her aux-iliary mothers. The rest of us separately went about our ac-tivities. This deviation from normal pattern when planning an assisticide salved our anxieties. I, for one, had begun thinking that our activities might best be concluded after Miss Pearl and Miss Ruby accomplished their end.

———

Sunday next was a glorious day, with the promise of a beautiful sunset. Miss Pearl and Miss Ruby hosted twenty-two guests with their 'Farewell to Summer' picnic.

Two long tables, clothed in ivory and deep red, were set with platters heaped with chicken, pork chops and ears of corn, all of them sizzling after having been roasted over glowing coals. Potato salads, coleslaw, sliced red tomatoes and snow-white cucumbers filled large green bowls beside them. Loaves of wheat and pumpernickel breads awaited slathering with fresh-churned butter, and baskets of polished apples at both ends of the tables invited crunchy bites. Beer by the bucket, of course, and tall pitchers of lemonade were served at their own stations. It was more feast than picnic, and summer's end was never more elaborately celebrated.

A third table, covered in white linen, supported two cakes that had been placed side by side and iced as one. A deep red candle centered one, and a taper of silvery cream had been placed in the other. Each candle bore painted flowers centered with glowing beads, pearl on the red candle, ruby on the cream, climbing from base to tip. Only Millie, of all the gathered here, had known this to be the day that marked the date of the twins' birth.

"Alpha and Omega," I breathed.

The timing of supper, cutting of cake, expressions of friendship, congratulations, and toast to long life were well planned. We sat together on the banks of the Lehigh River. Someone suggested singing 'moon songs', so we began with the one about the Man in the Moon being 'My Sweetheart' (very popular at the time) and went from there to other favorites. At the beginning of the day's end, when the sun's rays were just starting to diminish, Ruby spontaneously announced to Pearl that she would like to celebrate the day by taking a paddle on the Lehigh.

"What a grand idea!" was Pearl's light-hearted reply. "We aren't dressed for it, but that never stopped us before!"

So, with all their friends in attendance, these two astonishing women gathered up their raspberry silk skirt-pants, placed hand-above-hand to determine who would push off, climbed into their single canoe and glided out onto water whose welcoming surface parted into a pathway before them. They literally sailed onto the sunset, surrounded by reflected patterns of color that made way for their canoe, and then closed to embrace it, and them. When about fifty feet from the dock, they stopped paddling and uncorked a flask of their traditional brandy, poured from it into two silver cups, and drank a toast to each other. After this, they raised their refilled cups and drank again to all of us on shore.

They knelt low in their canoe, tossed both flask and cups into impatient waters, and waved good-bye.

"Paddle fast," I prayed.

The tragic passing of the Schumacher twins was noted far beyond the pages of "The White Laurel Times". Ruby and Pearl had acquired substantial fame as sportswomen and had garnered a degree of notoriety simply because they were women who had led unorthodox lives, and deaths, should the truth be known.

According to one published article, the pair had been observed trying to push their canoe away from The Lehigh's dam, but only succeeded in propelling it across. Their cry while they plunged into the pounding falls, as reported by a helpless onlooker, sounded oddly jubilant. He was waist deep in water, attempting to aid them, as their canoe had hung suspended, silent in space for only an instant, before disappearing toward the jagged rocks that swallowed it whole.

Ticket Number Seven and Ticket Number Eight

Millie's Mural

J ust about five weeks following the twins' departure on the train to Glory, all five of us gathered on Millie's third floor, before the doorway to a long, narrow room. Led by Millie, we walked onto a river. Water forming rapids over rocks, water forever flowing gently through widened passes, water supporting lives of fishes that leapt before us, water that flooded embankments and traveled beyond the boundaries of this room had all known the strokes of Millie's brushes as they were positioned on the floor. Instinctively, I raised my skirts and guarded my step.

And the walls, oh Lord, the walls. On them were permanently registered the perils and pleasures of Ruby and Pearl. They appeared in canoes painted at the bases of the walls, while the spaces behind them depicted scenes of their travels, as described by the twins to Millie. The sisters paddled past farmers' fields of hay, past hills awash with wildflowers, and through forbidding forests and jungles that let in little sunlight and held hints of danger. They traveled into yawning canyons of color created by high layers of rock rising all around them on either side of their craft, and along snow and ice covered embankments whose background was more snow and ice and bare, frosted trees. Their canoes ventured into roiling waters and onto placid ones. The twins were depicted as the people they were, determined and adventurous, yes, but they were also painted as curious, playful women. They were shown on shore in one scene making camp for the night before a blazing fire, and in another section they huddled under a tarp while rain poured around them. Another depiction showed the sisters running pell-mell from a farmer's surprised and angry cow, bell swinging as she charged the fleeing pair, while the rest of the herd calmly chewed cud. One wall revealed Ruby and Pearl holding on to each other for dear life as lightening flashed around them onto canyon walls. My very favorite depiction of all shows them dancing on a small island, frolicking sans costume, to the delight of a beaming Man-in-the-Moon.

In some of the scenes along the walls, Pearl and Ruby apparently had a guest. Dressed as the twins generally were, in bloomers and middy, a diminished Millie sat between them on a calm day and floated past a meadow full of daisies and Indian paintbrush. Blended into canyon walls, she helped to quell the fears of her friends. It was enchanting to find Millie's face in that of a fawn, or see her appear as a mermaid from a foaming wave, and delightful to discover her form in the shaping of a swaying tree. Millie appeared just about everywhere. Cleverly miniaturized, she fluttered among butterflies. Expanded, she formed the nucleus of a storm. The more we looked for Millie, the more of her we found. Daphne later remarked that Millie realized more adventure in her fantasy world than most of us do in reality.

The final section of Mildred Harper's work appeared at a point just before one's eye traveled back to the doorway. The waters now were those we could identify, and my breath caught. One's eye traveled across the painted river to the vast sloping lawn belonging to the Schumachers. Millie had brushed those of us present at Ruby and Pearl's farewell picnic into her mural. The lights and skyline of White Laurel formed her background. Afloat on the river in their canoe were the Schumacher ladies, dressed in their birthday garb, silver cups held aloft in farewell greeting. Lily, Iris, Daphne, and I were not pictured standing together, but instead were shown dispersed among the guests, each of us raising a glass in toast to the twins. Raised mugs foamed with beer. Tall glasses filled with lemonade were hoisted in celebration. Millie, and the four of us, held stemmed crystal in which floated liquid of amber.

Millie's Mural

Lily's Summons

By this time, we had become increasingly aware that detection of our activities could very likely occur. Already, we imagined that Doc Ramsey, after his comments on Mr. Lassiter's death, had some suspicions. Even though I suspected John might have made similar choices in his own practice, I could not expect him to overlook our performance of assisticide forever, even for me: I did not want to jeopardize the friendship that was growing between the two of us. My own thoughts were that we should best retire from assisticide and return to our whist. But one more plea, one that could not remain unanswered, came to us by way of our little coded bouquets.

Lily sent tussie mussies, ribboned with white, centered by a withered white rose and surrounded by lavender, basil, and red columbine. Oak leaves, commonly included in our nosegays, bespoke danger involved, while the rose suggested protection of innocence, and its neighbors indicated distrust, hatred, and anxiety. For the first time, a scarlet rose had been knotted into one of the ribbons. Lily had sent a cry for help, which none of us could ignore. We were to join her at noon.

That morning went by more quickly than I would have expected. Floraphile members arrived to clip spent blossoms from our profusely blooming roses, and I joined them at their task. Every lopped head sent a picture of this morning's tussie mussie to the forefront of my restless mind. At eleven, the ladies departed and I went indoors to wash up and change clothes for our meeting with Lily. I tarried a bit with Caruso (he was in fine voice) before concealing his yellow feathers beneath the cover of his cage. I checked the fire in the stove, placed the card in the window for the ice-man, and with a discomforting mix of feelings, walked the few blocks to find Iris waiting on her front porch. Hat in hand, she peered at me with questioning eyes, but I had no answers with which to assuage her. Slowly, while pinning her veiled hat onto her coiled braids, she came down her steps to join me on the sidewalk. Placing her gloved hand on mine, Iris kissed me on the cheek, and we proceeded on our way. Now, silence is not a customary companion to Iris and me, but on this day it accompanied our half-mile walk to Lily's old family home. As we came to the flagstone walkway that marked entry to the high wrought-iron gates, Iris spied Daphne approaching from the other direction. The speed of her gait caused Daphne's colorful curls to bounce around her head, and made her hat appear like a ship on high seas, steadfastly maintaining its balance. Ordinarily, we would have laughed aloud, but Daphne's face was clouded with the same concern we were experiencing, so we all linked arms and climbed the stairs to Lily's front porch. Iris had hardly turned the bell key before Lily flung wide the door and stood aside for us to file through her vestibule. Her naturally pale complexion had taken on an ashen tone, almost a match for the light blue dotted-swiss waist she was wearing. Uncontained wisps of Lily's pale blond hair framed her strong-featured face and gave even greater dominance to the expression in her eyes. She looks, I thought fleetingly, like a cornered, frightened rabbit.

After leading us into her drawing room, and thanking us for coming, Lily bade us sit wherever we wished, and rang the bell for Anna.

We sat, saying very little, while we waited. I focused on fine specks of dust hovering in beams of slanting sunlight, lazily rising and resting within eddies of the room's warm air. I studied in detail the pattern of roses and vines painted years ago by an itinerant artist who had decorated many of the walls in our town. I then concentrated on the numbers of borders in the oriental carpets, and was just about to count the candlesticks on the mantle when Anna's arrival with her tray of sandwiches and a pitcher of lemonade brought me back to the present. It had been awhile since I had seen Anna. She had become a truly pretty young woman, tall and graceful, with lovely bearing. I was rewarded with a dimpled smile from her tanned face when I spoke my thoughts aloud. Lily then told Anna that she could do as she wished with the afternoon, as Lily wanted to be alone with the three of us until five o'clock.

After Anna had closed the front door on her way, I supposed, to join some of her friends, I felt the air around us start to condense. Motes of dust settled onto whatever they encountered. The wall's roses and vines retreated into a distant jungle. Observing us with curiosity, Time had turned itself off while we waited for Lily to speak, and there was an infinitesimal period of nothingness before Time turned on again.

Lily appeared to be in another dimension, almost unaware of our being in the room, her eyes drawn together in concentration toward the tale still residing within her. Then, her voice broke the surface of our silence, sweeping from the depths of her being to inhabit the space around us. She began with obvious effort toward calm and control as if she were reading from a script, auditioning for a desperately desired role. I ached for her. Before two sentences passed her lips the script was abandoned and it flung itself across the room, beyond reach, no longer willing to be used as a prop. Lily's words became unrehearsed, tumbling across each other in their need for escape. They gushed from her mouth and became a river of spoken heartbreak, before coming at last to rest in pools of swirling letters.

She knew not, she said, just where to start, and so she just chose a place, then moved forward and back, but it didn't matter. Almost from the beginning, I knew the end.

———

"Years ago, when Anna's mother went back to Poland," Lily began carefully, "in order to join her husband and their aging parents, it was agreed that my mother and I would care for Anna until she returned. As you all know, Alice, whose Polish name is Alicja, never did come back for her child. Until recently there has been no word from her, over all this time. Now, as if she had walked away just yesterday, Alice has written that she is coming to White Laurel with her husband, and wishes to visit. I received her letter three days ago and have been out of my wits ever since. I just know that she is coming for Anna, to take her back to Poland, where I will never see her again!"

"What will happen with Anna?" Lily cried out. "Dear God, all I can think about is what might happen to her in the hands of that woman! She is still seventeen, just more than a child, and more mine now than Alice's! In truth," Lily said, as her voice dropped, "I have always considered Anna mine, from the time she was born."

At this, something shifted in my brain. 'Oh, God, I thought. Here it comes.' And then, it came.

"Almost eighteen years ago," Lily resumed in a voice so low that I needed to lean forward to hear, "when it became apparent that Alice was in a 'family way', my mother charitably sent her to be with Aunt Sophie and Aunt Sadie during her confinement. In turn," Lily spoke deliberately, "Alice was to assume all household duties for the two midwives until shortly before her baby's birth. But Alice fell from a stepladder two weeks after arriving at their home, and so I was sent, just before the end of the school year, to spend the summer in Mauk Chunk and help out. I adored being there with my aunts, of course, but did not look forward at all to attending Alice. Nevertheless, I arrived in time to," Lily had stopped speaking and simply sat there, staring at us – paralyzed.

Daphne and Iris started to rise from their seats to go to Lily's aid, but I bade them sit down again. Iris was clearly annoyed by my interference. Daphne was simply puzzled. Both of them looked to me for explanation, while I vacillated between suggesting that which I suspected and watching Lily struggle for strength to go on. Time watched urgently, having waited far too long for this moment. Lily, as if having been sharply nudged, cried out.

"I can't!" her voice rang. "I can't! I cannot lie or hold it inside me any longer! Anna was not born to Alicja that summer. She was never hers!"

"But Lily," Daphne quickly responded, her own thoughts not quite formed, "if Anna wasn't born to Alice, whose ba.. - Oh, Lily. Lily, she was your baby. Holy Mary, Mother of God."

She crossed herself and automatically did the same for Lily.

Iris, ever practical, got up and poured a good measure of brandy from a decanter on the sideboard, and handed the tumbler to Lily, with a nod to drink it down. She had just two words for our friend.

"Tell us."

Lily sat, staring at us, her wide eyes searching ours for anything other than censure.

Again, Iris' voice was a clarion in the room. "From the beginning, Lily."

"I fell in love," Lily began simply, as words of truth began to slip their bonds. "I, we, that is, fell in love. I was just about the age that Anna is now, and it all began when I was chosen to assist him in his office after school, an honor, truly, as his was most important work. Our becoming involved was the most beautiful and natural thing in the world, but he also loved his wife, and told me that he could not bear to hurt her; somehow, that made me love him all the more. He did not take advantage of me and my youth as one might think, (at this, I felt my whole body stiffen in indignation) as it was I who surely seduced him. He always said that it was my youth and beauty that unlocked the door to his foresworn desires, although I had never thought myself beautiful."

This, I found incredulous, and impossible to believe. Iris and I shot looks of mutual outrage to each other. If that man had been standing here in the room, I am hard pressed to say which of us would have throttled him first. Even today, Lily's obvious tenderness toward him was that of the child-Lily, for she had not seemed to advance beyond the convictions of her seventeen year-old self. No wonder, no wonder, I thought, as so many of Lily's oddities began to find resting places in my mind. Daphne looked over at each of us, her green eyes flashing with Irish indignation.

"We were together, in that way, only a few glorious times," Lily continued. I have tried again and again to convince myself that what we did was wrong, but have never succeeded in doing so. He, since he had a wife, and due to his profession of course, suffered terrible bouts of guilt, but I did not share them. I discovered that love blurs, and then allows for, what one has always considered unacceptable behavior. Sensibly of course, the man I still love to this day ended our liaison, and once more became faithful to his wife. I thought surely that I would die, so fierce was my pain, but I did not. Instead, a new life had begun within my body." Here, Lily paused, and asked Iris for a bit more brandy. She fortified herself, and did not stop again until she had finished her story.

"I wasn't sure, until my second monthlies failed to appear, that what I dreaded had actually come to pass. I was beside myself with the enormity of it all and just had to talk to someone, but felt that I could not possibly tell my mother – it would break her heart. So, in desperation, I told the woman who worked for us - Alice. To my surprise and immense relief, Alice listened calmly and without admonition. And then, she came up with a life-saving plan, the perfect solution. Together, we would make it appear that it was Alice who was expecting a baby. She would gradually add padding around her stomach, while I would begin wearing loosely fitted dresses. In this way her 'condition' could become known while my own reputation remained unsullied. Since we figured that the baby would be born toward the end of summer, I could most likely finish out the school year without anyone being the wiser. I could not believe my good fortune! Alice was a godsend! It never occurred to me that there was anything but my best interests contained in Alicja's proposal."

Lily had abandoned her glass of brandy to the marble topped table at her side. She spoke now with the directness of her profession, as if we were seated in her classroom.

"Morning sickness began during my third month," Lily confided. "Mother's concern for my health prompted her to schedule an appointment with Dr. Ramsey, and I knew that my pregnancy would be a secret no longer. So, fearing the worst but armed with Alice's plan, I told her why my daily upsets were occurring. I will not go into the extremes of emotion that my news produced. Suffice it to say that what hurt my mother even more than my pregnancy itself, was the fact that I had reached out to, and confided in, a woman other than herself. At first opposed to anything that our 'domestic help person' suggested, Mother reluctantly found herself won over by Alice's 'selfless' plan, and agreed to enter into it.

Sophie and Sadie, when contacted, readily agreed to be midwives to their niece, but they wanted Alice out of their home as soon as possible after the baby's birth. In fact, she could leave for Poland without ever coming to their home, and they would pay her way. They had long ago judged Alicja and wanted no part of her.

It all went like clockwork. Alice grew to be huge, while my condition remained hidden. Two days beyond her leaving for Mauch Chunk, I joined her there, on the pretense that she had taken a fall and my presence was required to 'help out'. My mother was praised for her Christian kindness to the foreign woman in her employ, and I received credit for selflessly going to her aid while missing my last few weeks of school. Directly after Anna was born, Alicja did sail for Poland, leaving 'her' baby in our care until she returned."

At this point, Lily became noticeably more agitated, and felt the need to rise and walk about as she spoke, before seating herself once more.

"What I did not know at the time," she said as she paced, "is that Alice demanded, and was given, a considerable sum of money for her masquerade. She had threatened my mother and her sisters that she would claim the baby and take her to Poland, as she could always give her away there, or sell her. Mother was horrified and sold a number of things that were precious to her in order to pay for Alice's silence. But Aunt Sophie had learned of threats of blackmail toward two of Alice's former employers, and her own subsequent warnings were enough to send Alice packing for Poland. Her passage was paid by Sadie and Sophie on the condition that she was never to return to America. One of my greatest rewards from teaching," Lily added softly "is that I earned enough money to buy back the cameo brooch that my father had given to my mother."

"And now, Alice is coming back," Lily exclaimed, "and she is not coming alone. She is bringing her husband! I am absolutely certain that she is going to claim 'their child'. That nightmare from the past will take over again, and it will be worse than before. I have not spent a full day, in all these seventeen years, during which I have not feared that this would happen. Anna does not know that she was born to me, to a girl who was not married. After all these years of her loving us, of having been told that her own mother had abandoned her, and then to learn that I am her mother – well, that just cannot be allowed to happen. Nor can she be allowed to meet this woman, this Alice, who is surely coming here to stir up a hornet's nest from which we all will be stung."

With that said, Lily picked up her glass, sipped at her remaining brandy while sinking into her chair, and waited for whatever response was to follow this revelation of hers.

We looked from one to the other as we absorbed our friend's story. Had Alicja, Alice as she was known here, not decided to come back to White Laurel, what we had just heard would undoubtedly have remained locked away within Lily for the rest of her life. Certainly, none of us would have wished to be in her place. Over the years, I had been involved in a few duplicities of my own. Surely Iris and Daphne had been as well. But none of ours compared to this one of Lily's. Hers was an absolute doozy. Why she had finally felt compelled to reveal her truths, we had yet to hear. I had uneasy feelings while I waited.

Daphne was the one to gather our thoughts and put them to the question. We had all seen the broom-straws that had been on the table since our arrival. Only on the day marking our decision to embark upon the one-way path of performing assisticide had a straw vote been taken. In a straw vote, Janeylib, a single straw broken beneath its covering napkin seriously challenges a presented petition. Two broken straws meant absolute abandonment of the proposal. Daphne deliberately faced our hostess and demanded, "Exactly what are you expecting of the three of us, Lily?"

Lily, who may not have understood Daphne's tone, immediately began revealing the plan she had devised to resolve her dilemma. During the time that Alice and her husband were in White Laurel, she proposed, Anna would go to visit Sadie and Sophie in Mauk Chunk, something Anna would love doing. While Anna was with the midwives, Daphne, Iris and I would receive dinner invitations, asking us to attend a reception for her two visiting foreigners. Lily would handle all of the preparations herself, and also do the serving; all we needed to do was attend, with our husbands naturally, if they could come.

Then, Lily sat back, apparently quite satisfied with whatever she had in mind, for a smile played with her features as she awaited our anticipated approval. After a few moments' time, that smile became a little less secure, as our combined silence began to perplex her. It was Daphne who again spoke for the rest of us. Her voice had taken on a sharper tone.

"What is going on here, Lily?" Daphne demanded of our hostess. "Just what are you saying that we are not hearing? I, for one, don't believe for a minute that you are simply planning an affair to welcome this former servant and her husband from Poland. From what you have told us, their presence in White Laurel could spell catastrophe for you and for your relationship with Anna. And why the wilted white rose in our tussie mus-sies?" Daphne was clearly agitated, to say the least, once again echoing the sentiments of Iris and myself.

"Whatever situation you got yourself into all those years ago," she went on with a finger pointed at Lily, "resulted in Anna's birth and a tangle of lies. You made your own choices and have lived with them, as has your mother, by the way, and you have submerged the true facts all this time. Now, they are all about to surface again, and you want us to be involved in some way. Just what are you up to with this dinner party of yours?" she asked heatedly, "and why would you even think of planning to have it? Are you proposing to serve up some precious poison in the potatoes of your honored guests? With us as participants?" Daphne sat back, staring hard at Lily, arms folded across her bosom.

"Not as participants, Daphne dear," Lily soothingly re-plied, in an attempt to ignore Daphne's indignation. "I simply request your presence as guests, but you have correctly read my intentions. Alice, and now her husband (if he really is her husband) must not be allowed to ruin Anna's life. There would be no end to their demands or their threats to Anna's welfare, so there needs to be an end to them. I see no other way. I do not intend to employ any of you in the execution of my plan, or to use any of our formulae, so you see, Daphne, none of you will really be involved at all. I have found a mushroom," Lily announced, clapping her hands together in delight.

Now mushrooms, as you may recall my saying, Janeylib,

were the one class of plant life we had ruled against. They were too readily detectable. Even worse by our standards, they were far too nasty. Some mushrooms actually carry a double dose of poison. Upon ingestion one becomes ill and then recovers somewhat, only to be felled by a secondary poison. Lily knew all about this, but was still willing to resort to using this mushroom she had discovered. Desperation had taken away her reason, I thought, as I anxiously waited to hear what next she had to say.

Lily was determined, as she repeated "I have a mushroom, one from which the victim does not die until at least a week past the time it is eaten. Often, ten to fourteen days go by without ill effect, so no one will suspect it as a cause of death. Oddly, this particular mushroom is found more frequently in Poland. Only rarely does its growth occur in Pennsylvania. I discovered some at the farm, had never seen any like them, and finally identified them after weeks of research. After a few trials, I found that minute amounts result in the delayed death of cats."

Lily looked positively smug as she continued outlining her devious dinner plans. The various courses she planned to present, and the ways she would ensure her guests consumption of these admittedly fascinating mushrooms was certainly well thought out, I must say. I sat there horrified but mesmerized as she went on with the fine points of her conspiracy.

"I will agree to pay their passage back to Poland," Lily said, apparently oblivious to our consternation, "and to further payments which I will send to them, provided that they leave immediately for home. It will be a most attractive offer, and one which they would be fools to refuse. Of course, they will never collect their future hush money. A week or so later, Alicja and her 'husband' will have departed not only White Laurel, but the rest of this world as well," Lily concluded. "Anna will not even know that they have been here," she added with a satisfied nod.

We were speechless, but Lily took no notice.

"Now," she went on, as she stood tall to do so, both gray eyes afire with purpose, "although I realize it is just a formality, I will pass the straws. I know this is a bit of a departure from our past endeavors, but it is Anna's life that we are rescuing." She smiled with confidence, as she picked up the napkin-covered plate to pass it among us.

"You can stop right there, Lily," Daphne called out decisively. "There won't be any straw vote today, and there won't be poisoned plates passed at any party that I attend! I am not going to sit here quietly while Iris, Flora, and I are subjected to this diabolical plot of yours. As I see it, it is your life we are saving, not Anna's. And I most certainly would not for an instant consider involving James in such a sinister scheme. That you choose to involve our husbands in this is appalling to me! The very thought of your expecting any of us to take part in this ruse to save your precious skin and supposedly protect your daughter just gives me palpitations!"

That said, Daphne rose like a rocket and pinned on her hat, ready to bolt for the door. I put a hand on her arm, delaying her departure, and faced our clearly shocked hostess.

"Daphne speaks for me as well, Lily," I told her. "What you are proposing as a mission of mercy is actually out-and-out murder. We don't commit murder. Assisticide, with every person we have aided, has been an act of deepest love and true compassion. There is a difference between assisticide and murder, and that difference is enormous. I truly think that desperation has robbed you of your normal capacity to think clearly. Surely, nothing other than loss of reason would inspire you to remotely consider such an insane plan."

Lily sank down dumbfounded, defeated, sinking into herself like a deflating balloon .

"Oh, dear God, you are right," she murmured as she stared at her hands. "Forgive me, please, all of you. I am so desperately sorry. How could I ever have come to this? I am so frightened for Anna, and just don't know what to do. What am I to do? I simply can't let Alice and her husband come here and destroy our lives. I just can't," and her eyes searched us for a solution, looking at each of us in turn.

Naturally, it was Iris, silent and absorbed for most of the afternoon, who provided the answer.

"Tell Anna yourself, Lily. Tell your daughter the truth."

That said, Iris, who was putting weight on again, pushed herself up and went to the door, where she paused for Daphne and me to join her. No further words were appropriate, and none was said. Anna was nowhere to be seen as we left her mother's house, leaving Lily to fathom the depths of her own being for her own answers.

As we clanged shut Lily's tall ornate wrought iron gates and stepped onto the flagstones, we reflected on the confession we had witnessed and the decisions Lily had now to make, hoping with all our hearts that they would be rational ones. Daphne turned off to go home to her children. I left Iris at her gate and waved to Walter, who was waiting for her at their door. Walking slowly toward my empty, memory filled house, my sharpened sense of separateness took me by surprise. Slowly, the reason for it came to me. Even Lily, I realized, had someone of her own to love. Perhaps it was time, after all, for me to acquire a pet, to have a dog in my house – or a cat – or one of each. Maybe two dogs, or two cats. No, two dogs and one cat. Yes, as I passed the gardens and approached my gate, two dogs and one cat.

Perfect enough, for now.

Alicja, never again referred to as 'Alice', arrived with her husband right on schedule.

All four of us were waiting there at the dock on that chilly September morning. It had been raining during the night and the sky had not yet cleared. Anna stood unsmiling at her mother's side. James, who had heard Lily's story from Lily herself and then been asked for his professional assistance in determining what to do, was there as well. We had journeyed to the coast the day before, had retired early, and as a joined band were ready to face Lily's nemesis.

We watched a surprisingly short and exceedingly stout Alicja descend the gangplank, her arm hooked through the elbow of a younger-looking man. She looked up in surprise as James officially approached, unbuckled his briefcase, and swiftly presented them with documents drawn up in both English and Polish. James had listed Alicja's past extortions and the consequences awaiting them should future transgressions take place, and then informed the stone-faced woman from Warsaw that their return passage to Poland had been arranged.

One thing I will say for Alicja: she wasn't stupid. One look at all of us standing together solidly behind Lily and her daughter, and another at the documents that James had prepared, resulted in her taking her obviously dumbfounded husband by the arm and marching off to the ship's steward to have their trunk reloaded for the return sailing to Poland.

The sun had begun to burn through the haze. Perhaps it was to be a fine day after all.

Lily's Summons

Mission Accomplished

By this time, I, personally, was scared witless that we would be discovered, perhaps had already been, and I was not alone. We had been unbelievably lucky so far, but it could only be a matter of time before some suspicious person decided to investigate further into the death of one of our passengers. When we began our mission, we each had our images of what it would be like to aid people who wished with all their might to leave this world for the next. We had contemplated, of course, in an abstract way, the dangers involved in providing tickets for the train to Glory. But now, living daily with the actual threat of discovery was becoming debilitating. Our days had become laden with the heaviness of the anxieties we all experienced. We will always believe in our cause. We will always be convinced of the rightness of our work. The consequences of the performance of assisticide, however, would be catastrophic for us and for those whom we hold dear, a dark fact that had become clearer and more frightening with each passenger's leave taking. We had been planning to put the brakes on our train to Glory for some time.

But what galvanized all of us, what put a mirror to our faces and a halt to our mission, was the insidious twist of mind that Lily had experienced. Realizing how dreadfully close we had come to having one of us commit murder sobered us like a flood of ice-water.

There was a second factor. Our lives were changing. Iris' weight gain, we learned, was due to a second miracle in her life, and her expected baby could not be jeopardized. As Daphne's James was becoming recognized in the legal world, Daphne's own involvement with the movement to gain the right to vote for women was requiring much of her time, and Lily was dealing with the repercussions of her revelation to Anna. As for myself, I joined Daphne in her personal passion to establish an amendment to our Constitution establishing voting rights for women. The fact that women have not had that right just makes my blood boil! On a personal note, my friendship with John Ramsey, who lost his wife two years ago, has begun to enrich my life in ways I had come to believe would not be mine again in this lifetime. I do not wish to place Dr. Ramsey in an awkward position should he discover proof of our work, and I do not want to lose his presence in my life.

We four blossoms, Daphne, Iris, Camas and Lily, have promised to be there for one another should the request be made. This is a pact we made at the outset, and is one we will honor.

Life in White Laurel is, as I imagine the world sees it, relatively placid - all of its attendant secrets kept quietly in drawers tucked among the stockings. Our own hidden truths are very likely not as exceptional as we would believe. We have most certainly learned more of life than we could have begun to imagine since our mission began. More importantly, we have come to realize that the word love is actually a verb.

Mission Accomplished

Afterlife

Sophie and Sadie are still living as I pen this account. It has become my great good fortune to come to know them well, an unanticipated dividend to my investment in our venture. I treasure the fact that their Brucie was the first to benefit from assisticide. My own two rambunctious pets are, I was assured, descendants of that cherished dog. A whole volume could be dedicated to Sophie and Sadie and their life's-work as midwives. Their service to women, and to men as well if truth be told, is worthy of a star in the heavens. I sincerely hope that they will one day reveal their own story.

———

Daphne's James stays, more and more, in Philadelphia. Their eldest son has become a lawyer himself, and is now married. He has not yet decided upon his father's offer of a position in his law firm, and Daphne strongly hopes that he will not accept it. Her reluctance to move from their home in White Laurel, she has confided, is not based on uprooting their younger children nor on her own desire to remain among us, but rather on James' dalliance with a young widow who sought his professional services. Apparently, she found them. Our Daphne is not, 'by all the Saints in Ireland' she claimed, willing to 'maintain appearances' by moving to Philadelphia and living an outwardly ideal life with her husband. James' image, she said, is something he needs to struggle with on his own. 'The stupid fool' Daphne calls him, a name she speaks in anger and resignation, as well as in love. I suspect this incident to be one among others, and the 'stupid fool' may very well be James' paramour, not Daphne's husband. Daphne is not about to relinquish her status as James' wife. But she has discovered a freeing joy in living on her own terms. Her household is fully staffed. Her children, nearly grown, are occupied with interests of their own. Our work has come to a timely conclusion. It had opened a gate, Daphne claims, to a world beyond her known one, and to blocks of time for her own explorations. Moving to Philadelphia for the sake of her husband's reputation would cause that gate to close, something she could not allow to happen. Recently, I asked her to preside over the volunteers who tend Norris Gardens, and she said no. She then surprised me further by saying that she had begun writing a book of poetry. I hadn't imagined that Daphne read poems, let alone wrote them. Like Millie with her murals, Daphne is unfolding before us all.

———

Lily is alone, at least for now, in that great big house.

Anna has moved herself out to the old Schultz-Lassiter place. I can only imagine the enormity of thoughts and feelings this young woman has to sort through, and the farm is a perfect place for her to be. She sent short letters one Wednesday to me, to Daphne, and to Iris, requesting our help and advice, and inviting us to a noon-day dinner the following Sunday. Of course, we accepted.

———

It was a betwixt day in late September, just enough warmth in the air to cajole me into thinking it a good day for walking, and I had talked Daphne into hiking with me to the farmhouse. Daphne was filled with the satisfaction of self-discovery these days, and on this morning she delighted me with what she wore. Her walking boots were topped by trousers cut long and full, and constructed from black and white checked linen. She must have sewn them herself, I thought, and Daphne smilingly nodded at my unspoken question. Slipping my arm through her green suede jacketed one, I whirled her around for the full effect of her figure in this wonderful costume. Well. Another plus for Daphne!

"I will make some for you, Flora," she said before I could ask, and off we went to the farm that was, at the moment, Anna's home.

The walk from town was not especially strenuous, but was of some distance, and both Daphne and I were grateful for the effects of exercise and autumn air on our minds and bodies. By the time we reached the farm, our appetites were making themselves heard, but we had made good time, for it was just past eleven o'clock. I was immediately impressed by the appearance of the old place. Anna had been busy with her weeks at the farm. Hired hands had shored up the front porch, and both house and fencing had been whitewashed, making them stand in panorama against the backdrop of woods up beyond the pasture. Windows glistened in front of old lace curtains, and the run-down old goat barn boasted patched walls and a fresh red exterior.

Iris, driven by Walter in his roadster, had already arrived and been lowered into a pillowed wicker chair. My childhood friend was roundly pregnant, their baby due to be born in just another month and a half. After going through months of anxiety, she and Walter had begun to relax, and today Iris was luminous. Bidding us sit with her before going into the house, she excitedly announced that she had really big news to tell us.

"Bigger than you are?" I teased her, and she laughed, wincing as she did so.

"Before coming here today," Iris told us as we sat down to listen, "Walter and I went together, as we always do, to my appointment with John Ramsey. On our last visit, Doc had half-jokingly remarked on my 'girlish figure', while frowning a little at my weight gain. Then today, as he listened for the baby's heartbeat, he frowned again. His face suddenly became serious, and he raised his hand to silence us when we began questioning. Our own hearts stopped beating," she said, "while we began to prepare ourselves for dreaded news. Then Doc looked up with a broad grin on his face, helped me to sit up a little, and placed the stethoscope's earpieces to my ears. "Have a listen, Mama," he laughed. While Walter stared anxiously at us, Doc looked over at him and smiled his round-faced grin. "There's more than one little rascal in there, you two love-birds!" he cried out. "My best bet is that you are the father of twins, Walt!"

Then, as Iris put it, "All hell broke loose. We laughed, we cried, we quieted down and listened again. Then Doc turned serious and asked if we would allow him to have an assistant with him at delivery time. Right away, I said to him, how about two assistants? I telephoned Sadie from Doc's office, and she called Sophie to the telephone to hear our news. They are arriving in another week and will stay as long as we need them. Forever, is what I told them, and we all laughed out loud."

———

So, that is how the two midwives from Mauch Chunk came to attend the births of White Laurel's first set of triplets: Sarah and Sophia, named in honor of the midwives who attended their births, and Walter, Jr. They were born perfect in every way. But, I am getting ahead of our story.

———

Anna, who had been standing at the door, spoon in hand, now invited us into her house. We helped Iris to her feet, and joined Anna in the comforts of her kitchen while she finished up with dinner. The room was brighter than I had remembered it. Jars of mums and late daisies had been set here and there, and the walls had gone from soft gray to a fresh coat of paint in butter yellow – how perfect for a kitchen!

"First we eat, and then, we will talk," Anna announced to our delight, as we sat down at her table and she picked up her ladle. "I know how hungry you all must be. Iris, please take the seat at the end of the table; it will give you a bit more room for the twins! Congratulations, by the way, and please be sure to call on me for help when they arrive!"

I marveled once again at Anna's maturity, so young and yet, so grown. Her dinner was both simple and outstanding. When I have made lamb stew, I have tossed potatoes into the kettle along with the other vegetables and simmered everything together. Not so our hostess. Anna's potatoes had been cooked separately, with sprigs of rosemary added to the water, then mashed with butter and cream and placed as nests in the bottoms of our bowls. Rich stew was ladled into the depression and sprigged with more rosemary from Anna's window-box. Fragrant combinations of lamb and root vegetables made their way from bowl to spoon to appreciative tongues. Anna had even made her own butter in Mrs. Schultz' (actually, Mrs. Lassiter's) old churn for the hearty brown bread she had taken from the coal stove's oven. Our mouths, too full of food to make conversation, were happy to be chewing. During dessert, a wonderfully tangy lemon-meringue pie, Anna handed around cups of tea or coffee, and began including us in her life. It is only fair that, as accurately as I can recall her words, I should at this point give Anna her own voice.

"First of all, before I begin, thank you all once again for joining me here today," began Anna. "I know how dedicated you have been to my mother, and in some ways, this visit may not be an easy one for you. It is not easy for me either, partly because I need to ask your help and possibly, your advice, neither of which I like doing," she said with a slight smile. "I have thought a great deal of my mother during my time alone here at the farm. In most ways, I have always thought of Lily as my mother. One of the hardest questions for me to deal with has been just whom she really thought she was protecting by lying to me all these years. At first, I thought, she was only thinking of herself. Later, I began to think that her silence benefited nobody at all. But then, little by little and then all at once, I realized that Lily protected every one of us by keeping the truth within herself: Nana, Sophie, Sadie, and, of course, Alicja, all were safe, and so was I. My grandmother, had the truth come out, would have been dismissed from her teaching profession under the cloud of scandal. Lily would never have been able to hold her head high in town, or permitted to become a teacher herself. I myself would have grown up, not as the daughter of a woman who had abandoned me, but as the love child of an unmarried woman. It is somehow still hard for me to forgive her, even though my own thoughts have begun to agree with hers. But this I must say, my mother's story is best left untold."

Anna looked to us for our support. I was truly pleased that she had allowed her mother this consideration, and was also proud of her for Lily's sake. There was no doubt in my mind that Lily's truths should be contained. Iris was the first to commend Anna's conclusion. I sometimes fail to recognize the natural wisdom of youth, and the courage that often attends it. Was I really so far from my own early years?

"How does your mother feel about your being here on the farm by yourself, Anna?" Iris then asked from her cushioned chair, as she shifted her weight.

"Lily has had no say in this, Iris," Anna said firmly. With an expression of authority I had not seen before, she continued to explain her position. "I simply had to leave that huge house and spend time by myself. Fortunately, I had this cozy home to settle in. Before Lily and I are together again, there are two things that will have to occur. So far, neither one has taken place, so I am acting on my own to satisfy my first demand, and may need your help. I am bringing my Nana here to the farm, to live with me."

Mercy, this was a surprise! Lily had placed her mother in private care because she couldn't adequately care for her herself, and now Anna planned to take over?

"The head matron at the Home had tears in her eyes when I told her what I wished to do," Anna said, "and she came from behind her desk to hold me in her arms. I would bring sunshine back into my grandmother's life, she said, although it is a huge responsibility, and she offered to assist me in whatever way she can. Almost everyone else at that place thinks that I have clearly lost my mind. We will see if they are right, but I truly think that we will be able to manage, and I know that I must try. I have arranged to have my grandmother brought here next week. If all goes reasonably well, and I just know it will, her move will be a permanent one. Hopefully, one day Lily will agree to Nana's coming home to the big house, but for now I will have her to myself. I can hardly wait, but do realize that I will need help and advice from time to time. I already had a telephone put in, and have hired a trained nurse to help for the first little while. Could one of you possibly be here with me for a few days when they bring her home to the farm? I know that this is a big thing to ask, but I'm not sure just what to expect. I would prefer that it be you, Flora, since you and Iris know her best, and I certainly can't ask Iris!" she added with a laugh. "No offense meant to you, Daphne, of course," Anna added. And Daphne tossed a dismissive wave.

"I will, most happily," I answered with no hesitation. "It will be my pleasure," I said, and I meant it. "Now, Anna, that issue is settled for the moment. You mentioned a second concern. Walter will be here in a few minutes to take his wife and babies home, so can you let us know what else is on your mind?" I already imagined the second requirement made of her mother. Daphne and Iris knew perfectly well also, but we needed to hear it from Lily's daughter.

She sat very still for a moment.

"There are two things that I presented to my mother after our day at the dock with the people from Poland. She needs to honor both things before I can begin a life with her as her daughter. One is the caring inclusion of my grandmother within our home. The second is in regard to my father. Not only must she tell me who he is, she must inform him of my existence. Each of us, my mother included I think, deserves no less."

"You have come far my dear," spoke Daphne, obviously impressed, "in a very short space of time."

"I have, Daphne, and by the way, thank you for allowing me to use your first names. Things are somehow working themselves out in my mind. Although it is still an enormous amount to absorb, I am profoundly grateful to know the truth, at least my mother's half of it. I still hope to know my father," she said, "and to hear from him what he has to tell me."

"Does Lily know that you intend to bring her mother here, Anna?" asked Iris, who then gasped as a foot or an elbow jabbed out within her.

"She does, Iris," as the doorbell announced Walter's arrival,"and she will be here herself for her first visit to the farm at the end of next week. After that, we will see what happens."

Afterlife

Finale

A nd so I end my penning of these pages, Janeylib. You, child of my heart, are beyond dear to me, and you need to know this – not just within your mind, but also within the flow of all that makes you alive.

Our lives here in White Laurel continue, but our final passengers have left the station on their trains to Glory, and we have been unbelievably rewarded for having aided their departures. We know in every fiber of our beings that this was appointed work. The strongest motivating factor, for us and for those whom our mission embraced, truly, was love.

We realize full well the legal ramifications of our deeds. We lived, and truthfully still live, with the very real fear of being discovered and exposed for the practice of assisticide.

Even so, what the four of us believe to be truly criminal is the denial of relief to those for whom there is no relief. Release from irreversible pain and torment, we feel, is one's rightful option. Hopefully, as these words are reaching your eyes, society will have grown enough in its wisdom to grant its blessing to the work we had to do in secret. What we legally did for Brucie should be an uncensored option for human beings.

Is there another reason that I was asked to write of our selves and about our mission? Actually, yes, there is. The rosemary of your wreath contains our message to you, my love. We want to be remembered for the work we have done.

Love to you forever,

Aunt Flora

Remembrance

I read my Great Aunt Flora's birthday gift for the first time lost in a state of suspended belief. Neither my brain nor my senses doubted the veracity of Flora's story and, when I began to really think about it, undertaking a dangerous mission if convinced of its justification is exactly what Flora would have done. Still, the enormity of what was unfolding before my eyes did not register all at once.

I read hastily that first time, eager to advance from one 'passenger' to the next and discover whatever would yet appear in this revelation whose pages I held. Gradually, as I learned of them, the age differences between Flora, her friends and myself silently evaporated. I was presently older than the women entering my world, and in my mind they became contemporaries. Save for the times that sleep would not be denied I became glued to the task at hand and could not wait, when I came to the end, to begin again. My days became centered and, without having realized that I had not been, so did I.

With my second reading, the words became pebbles lifting from the pages to find resting spots within me; I read with compassion so deep that my organs ached and my soul sighed. At times, I put the manuscript aside and went about my ordinary business of the day. I needed to do this to physically separate myself, to keep from disappearing altogether into the whirlpool of their tale. It somewhat disturbed me, this growing obsession to join them, but this second reading was far more compelling than the first, and read on I must. At some point all four women, indeed all of the people involved, began to make themselves at home around me, settling back on my worn leather sofa, peering out from behind the shower curtain, speaking to me as I stood at the kitchen sink. They were returning to life and indelibly permeating my own. Flora had told me at the beginning of her tale that I was known to all three of her friends. Surely, I recognized the woman represented as Iris, and must have met those known as Lily and Daphne. What had they foreseen that prompted their decision in choosing me to become the bearer of their secrets? This question is one I have pondered many times, and occasionally still do.

Perusing their words with greater reflection during my third reading, I allowed myself to enter their world as I had flowed into Aunt Flora all those years ago when I was eight, and learned that their story was not yet over. I was being entrusted to be a part of it. What these people could not do during their lifetimes, I realized with finality, I must do in mine. The wreath of rosemary and the blossoms it nestled was drawn for me, and I must make its story known.

I am now well past my sixty-fifth birthday. My children have children of their own and blessedly lead lives that are meaningful and expansive. Occasionally, I relieve the chemical professor at my alma mater, and my days go by quickly with volunteer and social events. I do not lack for funds, am of general good health, and do indeed feel blessed, because I am. But for a long time I had lacked a sense of solid purpose, some challenge that would require my own mental and emotional expansion.

Again, as she had done so often in my life, Flora was offering me an invitation to move beyond what I had considered a comfort zone and enter unfamiliar territory. I know very little of the world of publication and even less about promotion and marketing. I am about to learn, and in so doing promote myself as well, unfamiliar territory indeed. My mind is once more chewing healthy food that gives it exercise and I am more alive, with the experience of exploring realms once thought beyond me, than I have ever been.

I do not know where, or if, the saga of Flora, Iris, Daphne and Lily will end, but I knew that day as I slipped back into my own world where it must begin. I rose from the warm comfort of my couch, gathered the women's pages in my arms, and went to my purse for my cell phone. Flicking it open, I entered the numbers appearing on the business card before me and placed a call to Pennsylvania. After reaching her office and speaking with Lydia Wharen, Esq., I disconnected and began tossing things into a carry-on for my flight to Philadelphia. I found myself singing an old song my mother had taught me – 'my Sweetheart's the man on the moon – and I'm going to marry him soon....'

My own life was about to take off in new directions, and I was about to board a plane to Flora's favorite city – to share the revelations of the White Laurel Ladies for the first time, with Daphne's granddaughter.

The End

Author's Note: Although it is probably impossible to write a work of fiction without incurring similarities to someone living or deceased, the characters of Flora's Wreath are entirely fictitious. Although they became alive to me, and surely spoke to me from somewhere, none of them actually lived. The events portrayed in this book did not take place.

Guide to Group Discussion of Flora's Wreath

1. Many, many common indoor and outdoor plants are toxic; some are deadly. Angel's trumpet, for example, is aptly named. Accidental poisoning and death occur from contact with these toxins all too frequently. Does FLORA'S WREATH inspire you to learn more about this subject?

2. What is the significance of the character Brucie?

3. Would you like to communicate with tussie-mussies? Can you suggest ways, other than by using real flowers, in which they could be delivered?

4. Flora had a great deal of conflict concerning the assisticide of baby Luke. What are your views concerning this event? Can you empathize with Flora? With Iris? With either woman?

5. How do you view Lily's decision to shield Anna from the facts of her birth?

6. With which assisticide, if any, do you find it easiest to relate? And the most difficult?

7. I would love to spend time in Millie's aviary! How do you view Millie's decision to forego formal instruction at the Pennsylvania Academy of the Fine Arts?

8. Millie, Sophie and Sadie, Daphne's Mam and Gran, Pearl and Ruby Schumacher, along with Daphne, Iris, Lily and Flora took profound risks to accomplish what was important to them. Has this been a factor in your life?

9. Under what circumstances, if any, is assisticide justifiable? How do you feel about having a legal death with dignity option where you reside?

10. In what ways do you imagine Janeylib's life was impacted by the revelations made to her by her Great Aunt Flora?

CPSIA information can be obtained at www.ICGtesting.com
Printed in the USA
LVOW121602210312

274154LV00009B/90/P